Tales of the Gloaming

KATE SEGER

Soul of the Ocean

Rowan

"TAKE CARE OUT THERE, girl. The Wolves have been hungry on the High Road," the man whispered as he furtively placed the canvas-wrapped package into Rowan's basket. The packet contained a dozen crystalline vials filled with serum, the essence of life for her people. Contraband to the Lupine and their Celestial Overlords.

"You know I'm always careful, Henrí," she replied, though it was half a lie. Rowan was many things. Careful wasn't one of them.

She discreetly shifted the packet to the bottom of the basket, burying it beneath assorted other sundries. Then she pulled her scarlet hood over her head, obscuring her girlish features in shadow.

The city of Aeturnium glittered like a dark jewel as the man and the girl parted ways. Rain slicked streets shone like liquid onyx beneath the gas lamps. It was late autumn, and the damp chill was insidious, penetrating Rowan, burrowing into her bones.

She shivered and pulled her cloak tighter around herself. Walking at an even clip, she left the hulking tenements of Aeturnium's lower quadrant behind her as the inner city gradually gave way to rambling shops and villas. This was where she had to be careful. A young hooded girl running an errand on a rainy night was not unusual. But if a Lupine Enforcer caught the scent of the serum she carried–well, then she was as good as dead.

She kept her head down, rubbing the Wolf's paw in her pocket, hoping its scent would be enough to mask the coppery sweet aroma. The gate loomed up ahead. Rowan darted her eyes to the guard tower. Only two Enforcers were visible in the turret. Hopefully, they would be more interested in staying warm and dry than they were in her. She picked up her pace, left hand resting on the hidden bandolier of knives at her hip. Just in case.

But the guards didn't so much as glance at Rowan as she passed beneath the barbican and out onto the High Road. A little rush of excitement thrilled through her, the prickly jolt she always felt when she got away with something. She did a little skip and pressed on, following the wide road towards the ruins of Luxorna.

Before long, the thoroughfare narrowed, and majestic trees pressed in around her. She entered the Windwood, the primordial forest that formed a barrier between the Vampiric encampments in the Luxorna and Aeturnium, City of the Mortals. Wolves prowled the Windwood, Enforcers charged with "keeping the peace," another term for ridding the land of Vampires. Once, the Lupine Enforcers had steered clear of the road. It had been kept clear, guarded by the Vampires. But as their population declined, the Wolves took over, patrolling it night and day.

Rowan paused for a moment, considering. She could not outrun the Wolves in their feral forms. Ambushed on the open road, she had little hope of evading them. She would have to take her chances cutting through the forest.

Azriel

LIEUTENANT AZRIEL ULV sat in the tent, listening to the rain beat steadily down on the tarpaulin, twirling his dagger and dancing it between his fingers. He didn't really need the dagger. His wickedly sharp claws were weapon enough. But he'd managed to pick this one up off some bloodsucker, and he'd come to find this little game amusing.

He hadn't lost any fingers. Yet.

He put the knife down and took a swig from his canteen. Boris had swapped the water for hard cider, but Azriel couldn't help wishing it were something stronger. A nice Southport whiskey, perhaps. That might make this little game more challenging. And make the time pass more quickly.

He was bored and anxious. Their commander had been coming down hard on the Enforcers about meeting quotas. Apparently, bloodsucker smugglers were slipping through the cracks. But the Windwood had been quiet for days. If there were bloodsuckers out there, Azriel and Boris had yet to come across them. There had been that one old Vamp at the cabin, but Boris had taken care of her. Not a single sighting since.

"I'm going to take a piss," Azriel called to his partner, but Boris was already sprawled out on his army cot, snoring. "Lightweight," Azriel muttered under his breath.

He stepped out into the sodden, starless night. The cool air was sobering. He felt his fur begin to erupt in tufts beneath his jacket, protection against the stiff breeze. He had just unbuttoned his trousers when he heard the snapping of twigs and a muttered curse.

Azriel fumbled with the button on his pants, head whipping around. He narrowed his yellow eyes, pupils contracting as he scanned the forest. Fog ensorcelled the trees, hanging low over skeletal branches that clung to leaves of crimson and gold. He could see nothing through the damnable mist, even with his superb night vision. He had nearly convinced himself that he was hearing things when... there it was again. The sound of footsteps crackling over dry leaves.

A streak of red flashed in the shadows. Azriel growled low in his throat. He squinted, hypersensitive retinas scouring the dark terrain until he spotted a figure crouched about fifty feet away. A small huddled form in a scarlet cloak pressed up against the trunk of a hemlock tree.

Azriel prowled closer.

It was a girl, he realized. Young. Small. Just a slip of a thing, really. He remained motionless, watching, until she began to creep forward again, then he fell into step behind her. Lupines were fleet-footed, able to walk silently even upon the dense humus of the forest floor. Azriel easily closed the distance between them unseen, then circled around past her.

He waited until she neared his hiding spot, then stepped out into her path, calling out, "You there!"

The girl stopped, turning toward him. Her skin was pale and luminous, a fine replacement for the absent moon. Her eyes were downcast, but Azriel guessed that they were blue, the pale blue of the sky at first light.

He stopped himself. What kind of drivel was running through his mind? Too many nights alone in this accursed wood with only Boris for company. Too long away from Aeturnium and all its pleasures.

"Good evening," he said, keeping his voice low and non-threatening.

The girl stood frozen like a deer that had caught a whiff of the hunter, her body tense as a drawn bowstring as she stood there clutching her basket.

"Good evening, sir," she murmured, barely audible.

Azriel took a few steps closer. The rain was coming down harder now and he couldn't help but notice the way the girl's cloak clung to her body, intimating the curves beneath it. His pulse quickened, drumming in his temples. This was no child.

"What's in the basket?" he asked.

"None of your business," the girl snapped. Then she looked up at him.

Her eyes were indeed blue, but not the pale shade he

had imagined. They were the deep indigo of the sea at eventide.

Azriel swallowed hard and changed tact. "What are you doing out here in the woods alone? The High Road is a safer path for a–"

"Girl?" she interjected with a smirk. "I can take care of myself. I don't need a *dog* to protect me." She scrunched her face up, wrinkling her nose in distaste, then spat at Azriel's feet.

He blinked at her, his jaw falling slack. That's when he smelled it. The scent he was trained to track. Serum. The miasma of it washed over him, a coppery sweet tang so thick he almost choked on it. And the red cloak. Of course. This was no lost woman in the woods. This girl was a Vampire.

"As for why I'm here, I was hoping to avoid the lot of you beasts, but since you had to come sniffing around..." The girl's voice dropped off and her fangs darted out, white and sharp, sliding over the cherry red curve of her lower lip.

Azriel sucked in air with a hiss. His claws unsheathed, and he struggled to hold back his Lupine instincts. In feral form, he lost all control. He would shred this girl, tear her limb from limb. Which was exactly what he was expected to do. It was his job, his duty. But faced with this waifish bloodsucker and her fathomless blue eyes, he was disturbed to realize... he didn't want to.

The girl's hand flicked to her waist. Too late, Azriel noticed the knife flashing silver in the inky darkness. It soared through the air, end over end. Azriel tried to dodge the blade, but he wasn't quick enough. It lodged just below his hip with a sickening thud.

Azriel crumpled, grasping his wounded leg. His anguished howls echoed through the quiet forest as the girl took to her heels and ran.

He lay there for a few moments, stunned by the fire lancing up his thigh. He had to get up now. Before the shock swept over him completely, enveloped him in the darkness at the edges of his vision, left him unable to protect himself. Azriel staggered to his feet, pressing his body against a tree trunk for support and panting.

Get ahold of yourself. It's just a flesh wound. Forcing himself to steady his breathing, he shifted to his Wolf form. He could head back to the camp, but it was miles behind him. And Boris would give him shit for weeks if he hobbled back without the bloodsucker who'd done this to him.

He thought about the little cabin they'd discovered. The one where they'd found the old hag Vampire. It was close by. He could hole up there, at least until morning, and lick his wounds. With shuddering steps, he made his way through the forest, his mind racing.

What the hell had he been thinking? *Why did I hesitate?* The question nagged at him. Because she looked young, was beautiful? He'd killed hundreds of others like her before. But there was something about this one that he couldn't shake. Something about those blue eyes that tugged at his heart.

He forced his thoughts into submission as he

approached the cabin, his yellow eyes darting around as he scented the air. All was as they'd left it when Boris had driven the hag off into the woods.

He limped through the door. With the last of his energy, he collapsed onto the bed.

Rowan

BRANCHES WHIPPED Rowan's face as she tore through the forest, but she was too numb with adrenaline to feel the sting. She fought a rising panic shuddering through her guts. The wound had not been mortal. The Enforcer would be able to track her. If she led him to Luxorna, he would follow with more Wolves. It would mean death for her people.

Breathless, she paused, trying to steady her nerves and think clearly. Where else could she go? Not back to Aeturnium. The sun would rise soon, and there was no promise of safety for one of her kind in the city by daylight.

Lilith's cottage, then. The safe house.

It wasn't far from here. She could double back and hide there. The Wolf was wounded. If he came alone, Rowan would kill him. If he brought reinforcements, well, at least her people would be safe, even if the Wolves made an end of her. It pained her to think of the families that would starve without the precious serum she carried, but better hungry than dead.

She moved carefully, trying not to disturb the forest around her. The Wolf would track her. That was what Enforcers were born and bred to do. But she wouldn't make it easy for him.

As soon as she saw the cabin, Rowan knew something was amiss. The door hung ajar, its hinges shrieking as it banged in the wind. She inched towards the doorway, her hand tightening around the hilt of a knife. There was a dark smear across the pale wood timbers. She touched it and her fingers came away red.

Blood.

She pressed her body up against the exterior wall and peered inside. Even in the moonless dark, she could make out the trail of blood streaking the floor. Her eyes darted to the bed where a dark form lay curled upon the straw pallet.

"Lilith," she hissed, tiptoeing into the room.

No response. Had the Wolves gotten to her? Left her for dead in her own bed?

Savages, she thought, scanning the cabin's interior once more. There were no signs of a struggle. No one else seemed to be lurking in the shadows.

"Lilith," Rowan repeated a little louder.

Still, the figure curled in the bed did not answer. Rowan approached the huddled form. Her hands shook as she pulled the rough spun blanket aside, eyes squeezed closed, terrified of what she would find.

When she opened them, it was not Lilith's corpse she

found lying in the bed. It was the Lupine Enforcer. Unconscious.

Rowan knew she should flee. Leave him here to bleed out, or let Lilith take care of him when she returned. But lying there, with his eyes closed, dark hair swept back away from his regal face, the Lupine didn't look threatening. It didn't seem possible that this man—this beast—was an enemy dead set on destroying her.

She stood staring at him for a long moment. How had he known about the cabin? And where was Lilith?

The Lupine's eyelids fluttered, golden eyes opening to meet her gaze. Rowan expected to see loathing in them. They were mortal enemies, sworn to destroy one another, and he was lying there bleeding from a stab wound she had inflicted. Why wouldn't he hate her? But there was no menace in his eyes, only a flicker of fear.

And pain.

"So, you've come to finish me off," he said.

Rowan took a few steps closer. "It's you or me, right? Isn't that the way it's supposed to go?" she asked with a wistful smile.

The Lupine chuckled grimly. "That's the way of it," he said, resigned.

Rowan knelt beside the pallet and reached into her bandolier, pulling a knife free. Panic flashed across the Lupine's features. She ran with it for a moment, raising the blade as if she were about to stab him. A quick feint. Then, with a snicker, she turned the knife aside and sliced a long strip of fabric from the hem of her cloak.

"For your leg," she muttered, slipping the knife back into its sheath.

The Lupine's fists unclenched at his side, muscles visibly relaxing.

"What's your name?" Rowan asked. *Why?* she thought. *Why under the Celestials had she asked him his name?* This was getting stupid now. Dangerous.

"Azriel," the Lupine answered.

"I'm Rowan," she offered in return, knowing she should not, recognizing this was insanity, doing it anyway.

"Like the tree?"

She yanked the makeshift bandage she was winding around his leg hard enough to make him wince. She hated stupid questions. "Obviously," she deadpanned.

Then she reached into her basket, pulled out a loaf of bread, tore it in two, and thrust half at him. "Here. Eat it," she ordered.

The Enforcer shot her an uncertain look but took the bread. They sat in awkward silence, gnawing on fresh bread and listening to the thrum of raindrops upon the thatched roof.

Where is Lilith? And what would she say when she returned to her cabin and found Rowan giving succor to this Lupine?

Rowan

ROWAN WATCHED THE LUPINE STRIP, fingering one of her blades. He unbuttoned his uniform jacket and removed it, along with his white-collared shirt. She should be repulsed. This was a Lupine. A disgusting, murderous beast. Instead, she found herself strangely drawn to him.

He was tanned and well built; his musculature defined but not bulging like some of the Lupine she'd seen. Only a sparse tawny dusting of hair covered his chest. She flicked her eyes over the smooth ridges of his abdominal muscles, tracing the line from his navel down to his belt buckle.

"Those too."

Azriel scowled at her but obeyed. He dropped his camouflage pants, revealing white undershorts and powerful, chiseled legs. A trickle of blood seeped from the wound in his upper thigh. Rowan's mouth watered.

"I expected you to be hairier," Rowan said coolly

when she'd finished her appraisal.

Azriel smirked. "Sorry to disappoint."

Rowan took a few steps closer to him. The smell of his warm blood coupled with his state of undress was tantalizing, almost irresistible. Her fangs slipped out over her full lips. "I'm not disappointed at all."

"What are you doing?" Azriel asked, taking a step backward. He winced as his weight fell on his bad leg.

"Just looking. I won't hurt you," Rowan crooned.

She stopped about a foot away from him. Bloodlust sent an endorphin rush through her. Serum would put a stop to that, but she found herself not wanting it to end.

"Do you find me revolting? Disgusting?" she asked, removing her scarlet cloak and letting it slip from her shoulders to pool on the floor at her feet. Beneath it, she wore a skintight black leather bodysuit. It was more for practical purposes than anything else, made for skulking about in the shadows. But she also knew the effect the ensemble had on men.

Azriel appeared taken aback. For a moment, he only stammered, "What? No. I mean, I think—I think—" He dropped off.

He was *blushing*, Rowan realized, amused. She felt color rise in her own cheeks.

"Do you want to touch me?" Rowan inched closer to Azriel. She watched his Adam's apple bob as he swallowed. Reaching, she took his hand in hers. Her fingers were small and pale as a porcelain doll's beside his. She drew his palm to rest on the soft swell of one ivory breast.

"I—uh—" he choked out.

A vicious little smile toyed at Rowan's lips. "I want to taste you," she breathed, her pink tongue darting out over her fangs.

Azriel shifted in a vain attempt to break away, but Rowan was strong despite her fragile physique. Her hand snapped in a vice-like grip around his wrist.

"So, you only spared me to play with me, to make me suffer. Why not make it quick? Be merciful, kill me, and be done with it. No more of these games," Azriel growled.

Rowan cocked her head again. Her eyes hardened, and she released his wrist. "No, I don't think I'll kill you. At least not yet," she drawled. "I know I should. But I find you... interesting."

Azriel rubbed his wrist where her long nails had dug into it, drawing blood.

"I mean, besides, you're wounded, and it wouldn't be sporting."

The Lupine rolled his eyes. "Your kind never cared whether the fight was fair before. You see a Lupine, you kill a Lupine... unless they kill you first."

"My kind," Rowan spat. "Did it ever occur to you that not all Vampires are the same? That we're not all blood-sucking fiends any more than you're all mindless beasts? We're just people trying to survive in a world where we're hunted just for having the audacity to be born."

Azriel's jaw went slack. Perhaps it really never *had* occurred to him. "Get dressed," Rowan ordered.

For a long moment, Azriel only frowned down at the robes lying on the ground. Rowan watched him closely. His muscles tensed. He was still waiting for the death blow, the fool. Finally, he snatched up the robes and pulled them over his head. Rowan couldn't help but giggle. They were ill-fitted, too short by three inches at least. But that shouldn't be a problem. Most Vampires wore hand-me-down robes. They could afford little else. Fortunately, the voluminous cut did well enough to hide his muscular body.

"What are you laughing at?" Azriel grumbled, which only made Rowan erupt into an even more intense burst of giggling.

She covered her mouth with her hands, trying to force down the giddiness. "Nothing. Put on the cloak, and let's go," she said, a little breathless.

Azriel toed the red cowl, scowling. "What is the point of this whole charade? Haven't you humiliated me enough?"

"I'm taking you home with me," she said with an innocent flutter of her thick eyelashes. She retrieved her own cloak and fastened it at her throat, pulling the hood up to conceal her face.

Rowan had no idea what she'd do with him once she got him back to Luxorna. She could turn him in to the council of Elders—should—turn him in to the council... but there was something about him. Perhaps she'd play with him a bit more before she turned him over.

"Let's go," she barked, nudging him between the shoulder blades.

Azriel

IN THE MORNING, weak rays of sunlight filtered through the cabin's single window. The air smelled musty and copper tinged; the scent of his own blood mingled with the damp earth of the dirt-packed floor.

Azriel did not remember falling asleep. He remembered the bloodsucker, but she was nowhere in sight. Perhaps the girl with the dark hair and red cloak had never been there at all. Perhaps his leg wound had festered, and it had all been a fever dream.

He winced as he sat up, a shock of agony shooting up his thigh. Inhaling sharply, he bent to inspect the wound. It was still bound in a strip of red cloth.

So, it had not been a dream after all.

Azriel lurched to his feet, grinding his teeth against the pain as he stood, ready to limp back to the encampment with his tail between his legs. Boris would never let him live this down. He'd gone off to take a piss and...

He had just begun the transition to his Wolf's skin when he smelled it.

Serum.

He glanced to his left and saw the Vampire standing in the doorway. Her hood was thrown back, and raven locks fell around a delicate, heart-shaped face. She looked to be little more than a child, but he knew that her appearance was deceiving. This was a woman grown, armed to the teeth, and a bloodsucker. Not someone to underestimate, despite her stature.

"I can't let you leave," she said.

"You ought to have killed me last night," Azriel growled. "So I didn't have to wake to this misery." He glanced at the gory bandage around his thigh.

In her right hand, the one that wasn't resting on those bloody knives of hers, the girl—Rowan, that was her name—held a small basket.

"This is for your pain. Drink it," Rowan said, releasing the knife to rifle through the basket. She pulled out a small crystal vial.

"Why bother? Your Elders will just torture me when you turn me in. I might as well get used to pain. That is your plan, isn't it? To turn me in?" Despite his grumbling, Azriel took the vial from her and examined it.

Rowan cocked her head to one side, watching him as he gulped down the contents of the vial. He immediately felt relief, the shooting pain becoming a dull, aching throb. Bothersome, but not as unbearable as it had been. He blinked twice as unsettling energy flowed through his veins. If it was poison, at least it was a sweet one.

"It is my duty to bring you back to the Lair," Rowan said.

"I'd rather die and rot than be put to the question by a bunch of bloodsuckers," Azriel snapped.

"Where is Lilith?" Rowan asked, changing the subject. She leveled her gaze at him, and Azriel marveled again at the startling blue of her eyes. He felt like he was plunging down into a deep azure sea when he stared into them.

Struggling to drag himself back to the surface, he asked, "Who?"

"Lilith, the Vampire who dwells in this cabin," Rowan reiterated a little impatiently.

Azriel groaned inwardly, his mind lurching through several fits and starts before he spoke. Most likely, the old bloodsucker was dead. Boris had said he'd "taken care" of her. But if he told that to the girl, he'd wind up with a blade through his gullet before the words were even out of his mouth.

"I have no idea," he lied.

Rowan assessed him, then strode over to a chest of drawers. She pulled out some voluminous white robes and battered scarlet cloak, similar to her own.

"Put this on," she ordered.

Azriel stared at her, dumbfounded. "I'm not wearing that," he protested.

"Then I'll have to kill you, I suppose." Her hand dropped back to her bandolier.

Azriel

HOME. Azriel's blood went cold. The bloodsuckers resided in encampments in the ruins of Luxorna. Once the twin city to Aeturnium, it had been demolished when the Celestial Overlords had learned exactly what kind of plague they'd released within its walls. Now a bastion of the Vampires thrived there, gorging themselves on the blood of bats and rats to sate their unquenchable blood lust. Or so it was said. Azriel didn't know any Lupine who had been to Luxorna—and made it out alive.

He took a couple of steps towards the door, then stopped abruptly. "Wait, can you go out in the—"

"Sunlight?" Rowan finished for him, nodding. "Why do you think we wear these red cloaks? It's certainly not for camouflage. They're woven from bambana root. It protects our skin from the sun's rays. But don't go getting any ideas that you can best me by stripping me of it. We burn in the sun, it's true, but I think you'd be surprised at how long it would take to weaken a Vampire as old as I am."

Azriel wondered how old she was. One hundred? Five hundred? A thousand? Vampires could live for millennia if they didn't starve, burn, or have a stake—or a claw—driven through their hearts.

"Let's go," Rowan ordered again, pushing him from behind.

He had no choice but to oblige her. He couldn't outrun her, even in his Wolf form. Not with the wound in his leg, and weak as he was from blood loss. If he fought her, she would kill him. Perhaps the forest would provide an opportunity for escape. Perhaps Boris would manage to track him down and come to his aid.

They left the cabin and headed out into the woods. The previous night's rains had stopped, but the air was still heavy with humidity, the forest floor dense with fog. It was like the ghosts of the previous evening had failed to return to their graves with the breaking of the day. The trek to Luxorna was long, and Rowan walked behind Azriel, urging him forward, seemingly indifferent to his wounded leg.

"Why do your people hunt us?" Rowan asked abruptly. Azriel stopped walking and turned to stare at her.

"What?" he asked, taken aback by the question.

"Why do the Lupines want us all dead?" she repeated. Her tone was casual, but her eyes were steely, their indigo seeming to darken with her mood.

Azriel looked away and fidgeted with the frayed hem

of his borrowed cloak. He cleared his throat, hoping she would relent in this line of questioning and push on. Hoping Boris would erupt out of the forest with a band of Enforcers and spare him this conversation.

"You are unnatural," he finally forced out.

Rowan's dark eyebrows lifted. "Unnatural, you say. And who made us this way?"

Azriel averted his eyes, fixing them to the forest floor again. Gods, why must she do this. Everyone knew the bloodsuckers were the Celestial Overlords' creation, but they were an abomination. That was why the Lupine had been created, to put an end to the Vampires' foul unnatural existence. Or try to, at any rate.

"If Luxorna hadn't rebelled, the Celestials would not have had to release the plague. But Luxorna rebelled. And now you're all cursed, plague-ridden, unworthy of life." Why sugar coat it? Surely the girl knew the history of it all. This was just more of her taunting.

"The Overlords created the Lupine as well," Rowan countered.

"We are Enforcers of the Light. Vampires are creatures of darkness."

Rowan only snorted at this, then jammed her fist into his spine. "Get moving." She gave Azriel a hard shove.

It was about an hour later when Azriel's head suddenly started throbbing. His vision blurred, and little stars pinpricked behind his eyes. He stopped in his tracks, causing Rowan to crash into him. Slight as she was, the impact was still enough to make him stagger and fall headlong to the ground.

His vision went black. He could hear Rowan cursing, dimly, as if she were a world away. He felt the sting as she slapped his face but could only moan in response. Something cold touched his lips. Reflexively, Azriel swallowed. A thick, viscous substance that tasted salty yet metallic coated his throat. The same thing he'd been given in the cabin, he realized. He coughed, a quick spasm of convulsions, then his eyes shot open.

"What is that stuff anyway?" he choked out. There was a surge in his body again, like lightning shooting through his veins. He shuddered as the unshakable energy coursed through him.

Rowan held up the vial, half full of a thick golden liquid, grinning. "Serum," she said.

Serum... Alarm bells rang in Azriel's mind. Serum was the foul drug the Vampires used to maintain their immortality. A synthetic substance made from the antibodies in mortal blood. He coughed and spat, his stomach turning. To drink serum was a crime, punishable by years of imprisonment in a Lupine Gulag. If he tested positive for it back at camp...

"I wasn't sure if it would work on your kind. But it seems to have the desired effect. A boost of energy and strength. Pain killing properties. Perhaps we're not so different after all."

"But it's banned. It's illegal," Azriel sputtered.

Rowan rolled her eyes. "You Lupine and your bloody

laws. It's not illegal in Luxorna, and that's where we're going. Don't tell me you don't feel better."

The truth was, he *did* feel better. His leg still pained him, but it was just a dull ache. And now that the initial strange rush had worn off, he felt stronger, too.

"I do," he conceded, "but—"

Rowan cut him off. "Good, then get up. They've probably sent someone out looking for you by now." She nudged his shoulder with her boot.

Azriel scowled and rose cautiously. His head didn't swim, and his vision remained clear. He considered using his newfound strength to escape. But the odds weren't in his favor, and much as he hated to admit it, the idea of seeing Luxorna with his own eyes intrigued him.

He began to walk.

The sunset was alighting over the mountains in a blazing red and gold display when they finally reached Luxorna. Rowan reached up and pulled Azriel's borrowed cloak farther forward to better conceal his face.

"Keep your head down. Talk to no one. Look at no one, just walk," she hissed, moving to flank his left side. She took his wrist in her vice-like grip and urged him forward.

Side by side, the Vampire and the Lupine strode through the crumbling gates of the ancient holdfast of Luxorna. The streets were silent as they passed beneath the fallen arches into the relic of a city. Their footsteps echoed as they passed abandoned buildings towering like massive sarcophagi over the shattered streets.

But no... not abandoned. Azriel saw these buildings were occupied now. Pale, ragged, red-cloaked forms huddled in doorways. Gaunt faces with haunted eyes peered out broken windows at the duo as they passed. A woman with an open door stood hunched over a burning trash can, a small animal, likely a rat, roasting on a spit. She looked up as they passed, fangs sliding out over her chapped and bleeding lips.

"Are all Lupine as rude and foolish as you?" Rowan growled. "I told you not to look at them. *Don't draw attention to yourself.*"

A firm elbow in his ribcage forced Azriel's eyes back to the street. He still felt strange from the serum. Energized yet shaky. Every color looked brighter but also hazy. As if he were walking through a dream. Or a nightmare.

Rowan led him towards the broken corpse of a temple. It soared heavenward and seemed almost to kiss the clouds, but like everything else, it was crumbling. Several of the tall pillars were cracked down the middle, and fragments of gold-flecked marble littered the ground at the entrance.

Azriel's heart began to thud harder in his chest. As if she sensed it, Rowan squeezed his hand gently.

"I'll protect you," she said with a smirk.

Azriel rolled his eyes, following her with hesitant steps into the desecrated building. Most of the stained-glass windows were blown out, but a few remained intact. They depicted fanciful scenes of an age long gone when the Goddess reigned over all Astrium. When neither Vampire nor Lupine had been born yet. Sunlight filtered through, bathing the room in a strange reddish glow.

They passed rows of splintered pews carved from white willow as they walked down the aisle towards a large golden altar. Rowan approached it. She reached beneath a tattered cloth-of-gold altar cloth and fussed around for a moment.

There was a sound like gears in desperate need of oil grinding. Azriel watched with wide eyes as the altar began to sink down into the cracked tile floor. When it vanished, Rowan stepped down and disappeared into the hole. Azriel peered after her into the deepest darkness he had ever experienced. He could see there was a rope ladder descending into the abyss, but beyond the first five or six rungs, even his keen night vision could not permeate the darkness.

"Hurry up, I can't leave it open all day. They'll get suspicious," Rowan's voice filtered up, echoing off the stone walls.

Azriel took a deep breath and entered the hole. He felt the ropes straining beneath his weight. Having no idea how long the drop was, or what lay beneath him, he could only pray the ladder held his weight. Twenty rungs he went down, then thirty, then forty. Finally, he could see a flickering blue light beneath him and knew he was nearing the end of his long climb. Once his boots finally struck solid ground, he released the breath he hadn't realized he'd been holding. He turned around to get his bearings. Behind him, the altar. Before him, Rowan.

She stood holding a bronze oil lamp in her hands.

Blue flames danced on the wick, casting shadows on her pale face. He was taken again by just how beautiful she was, with her unnaturally pale skin, lips glistening red as roses, slightly parted, watching him with an intensity burning in her eyes.

"Why did you bring me here, Rowan?" he asked.

A shadow of uncertainty passed over her eyes. "I want to show you what your people have done to us," Rowan said, a touch of bitterness creeping into her tone.

Azriel flinched at the sharpness in her voice, but Rowan didn't seem to notice. She reached across him, fingers brushing across his chest, and pressed her hand against a small indentation in the rocks. There was a rumble, and the altar began to rise, sealing the shaft they'd climbed through. Rowan turned on one heel and set off down the stone corridor.

Azriel hesitated for a moment, pressing his palm against the wall as Rowan had, eager to understand the trick. Nothing happened.

Before he could investigate the curious mechanism further, Rowan called out to him, "You'll have to find your way out alone in the dark if you don't keep up. And I promise, it will take you a long time so and there won't be a warm reception when you emerge."

Azriel cast another curious glance at the strange impression in the wall, then hurried to catch up to Rowan's blue flame. The passage was narrow and winding. Azriel tried mentally to mark the turns they took down various side corridors, but quickly lost track. Down here, it smelled faintly of mold, and the soft drip...

drip... of water running through channels in the walls was audible. It was only a matter of time before the fissures expanded and these passages collapsed. Azriel hoped he wouldn't have the misfortune of being down here when it happened.

They emerged into a large chamber. The vaulted ceilings were painted with celestial images and torches were inset in the wall. Rows of sarcophagi sat neatly arranged side by side.

"Keep your head down, hide your face. If we're lucky, they'll be too hungry to notice anything amiss about you," Rowan hissed.

At first, Azriel wondered who she was talking about. He didn't see anyone, and he was preoccupied with this incredible space. So, the Luxorna Catacombs weren't just a myth. They actually existed, just like in the stories he'd been told at his nursemaid's knee.

Then his gaze caught on a pair of round eyes peering out at him from the shadows. Someone, a child, emerged from a sarcophagus. No, not just one child... many children. They climbed out of the stone caskets and melted out of the shadows, all of them pale, ethereal, and emaciated-looking.

"Rowan, did you get it?" a spindly boy with silver hair and icy blue eyes asked. Rowan smiled warmly at the child, reaching into the basket she carried and pulling out one of the small vials. She handed it to the boy, and the rest of the children rushed forward. They tugged at the hem of Rowan's cloak, reaching out with small, grubby fingers. A few cast uncertain glances at Azriel's hooded form, but most were so desperate to get hold of the vials that they paid him no attention whatsoever.

"There are only ten," Rowan said, trying to hide a grimace. "Some of you will have to share."

The children did share. When Rowan handed one to a young girl with a long scar running down the side of her face, the child drank half, then handed the rest to a younger boy who must have been her brother. He downed the rest.

"Now, don't linger here. It's too close to the surface," Rowan gently chastised the children. They whined and chattered for a moment. Rowan's face grew stern. She pointed down one of the tunnels, and the children scampered off, their footsteps echoing in their wake.

"The serum—" Azriel began, but Rowan drew a finger to her lips and hushed him. She squinted down the tunnel, cocking her head as if listening. When she seemed satisfied that they were out of earshot, she turned back to face him.

"The serum, the foul drug your leaders so abhor, is for the children. And the sick or wounded. Healthy adult Vampires feed infrequently. We can survive on the blood of bats and rats for a great many years. But the children... without mortal blood or serum, they starve, waste away, lose their minds with hunger," Rowan said. "A starving young Vampire is a danger to us all. My people as much as yours."

Azriel's stomach knotted as he thought about all of those hungry-eyed Vampire children.

"Let's go," Rowan said, nodding her head towards a

tunnel running opposite the one the children had disappeared down.

As they walked, the corridor gradually began to widen and slant upwards. They were heading back towards the surface, Azriel realized. He breathed a sigh of relief. He couldn't get out of these catacombs soon enough. The dripping of the water set his nerves on edge, and the faces of the children were emblazoned on his mind. Poor wretched starving things secreted away in this dark underground world intended for the dead.

The air began to lose the musty, damp aroma, growing fresher. Up ahead, a faint tracery of light surrounded what could only be a door to the outside world. Rowan was about to push it open when Azriel took her by the shoulder and spun her around.

"Rowan. Why have you really brought me here?" he demanded.

Rowan

WHY HAVE *you brought me here?* The question caused Rowan to freeze, her hand hovering on the door handle. Why *had* she brought him here? What did she hope would come of dragging this Lupine back to Luxorna, down into the catacombs where they kept their young?

She hadn't thought this through. Hadn't thought it through at all. She had just acted on impulse. Like some shiny thing that caught her eye, she'd snatched him up and brought him home with her. Seven hundred cycles, and she still hadn't learned to think before she acted. *Now,* what was she going to do with him? She couldn't just send him back to his detachment. Not when he knew their most closely guarded secrets. And she couldn't stand the idea of turning him over to the Elders either.

"Rowan?" Azriel repeated her name, and she blinked, forced back to herself.

"I wanted you to see," she said. "To see what the Overlords have done to my people. What the Lupine have done to my people."

Azriel opened his mouth to say something, closed it again, and scratched at the dusting of stubble on his chin. "I'm sorry, Rowan," he finally said. Because, really, what else *could* he say. "And now that I've seen? Will you turn me in? Complete your revenge? Send me to the Otherside with a guilty conscience?" There was a touch of fear in the Lupine's eyes, but also resignation. He had been waiting for the axe to fall from the moment she'd found him in the cabin.

"Not right away," she said breezily. "I've never had a Lupine at my mercy before." When she smiled, her fangs slid from their sheaths. She pushed the door open. "Same as last time. Head down. Don't draw attention."

They stepped out into the crisp autumn day. The flute-like melody of a wood thrush's song carried on the air, high and sweet and a little forlorn. The tunnel had put them out on the southern fringe of the city, not far from Rowan's home. She would bring the Lupine there, then figure out what to do with him.

Azriel followed without being ordered and kept his head down. After a couple of blocks, Rowan turned left down a narrow lane. This part of Luxorna had once been suburbs in the days before the Overlords had sacked the city and loosed their plague. The broken-down apartment buildings were replaced by dilapidated manor houses here. Most Vampires felt safer huddled together in the guts of the city. Many of the houses in this district had been long abandoned.

But Rowan hated the press of eyes in the city center, the way they all gazed at her with desperation. *Save us*, their looks seemed to beg. But she could not. She could barely obtain enough serum to feed the children. So, she had made her home here in what had once been the garden district. Even now, roses climbed the trellises that leaned over flower beds gone to seed. They, too, struggled to eke out a life in the ruins.

She wondered if Azriel had noticed that the city was a mirror image of Aeturnium. Sister cities. Twin cities. One risen, one fallen. She made another left, Azriel following dutifully, then strode up to the entrance of a burnt-out manse.

"Welcome to my home," Rowan said as she inserted a small brass key in the door and turned the knob.

She gestured with a flourish for Azriel to enter, and he brushed past her into the house. He was limping noticeably, and his face was set in a grimace. The second dose of serum was wearing off.

He took a seat on the worn sofa that had once been quite the elegant furnishing. Now it was threadbare. Elegance was a luxury that no one in Luxorna could afford. Rowan sat down across from him on a small stool.

"Here," she said, rummaging in her pockets and pulling out a small vial containing the other half of the serum she'd given him in the forest. She moved to hand it to him, but Azriel shook his head.

"Save it for the children," he said through clenched teeth.

"Why?" Rowan blinked at him, startled. For the children? These children would one day grow up to be the same creatures Azriel and his brothers hunted in the Windwood. Vampires like her. Why would he want to save them?

Azriel shrugged and didn't answer. There was weariness and pain in his eyes. He shifted on the couch, propping his wounded leg up. Unfastening the long red cloak, he tossed it aside, then pulled the white robes off over his head. He reclined on the sofa clad in only his undershorts and closed his eyes.

Rowan knew she should look away. There was a forced intimacy here that she found unnerving. But she could not pull her eyes from his lean, muscular body. Her gaze roved over him, stopping at his thigh, which was smeared with blood that had leaked through the makeshift bandage. Rising, she padded to his side and knelt beside him. Azriel's eyelids cracked open, his gaze locking with hers.

"Drink it. Please," Rowan insisted, holding the vial out.

Azriel opened his mouth and started to say something, but she stopped him, bringing the vial to his lips and pouring it into his mouth. He spluttered, but swallowed.

"Why?" This time it was Azriel questioning the inexplicable. "Why do you care if I'm in pain? You're supposed to hate me, to want me dead."

Already Rowan could see the tension leaving his face as the pain grew more manageable. "Because I wanted you to have it," she answered simply.

Azriel brought his hand up, moving it to Rowan's cheek. When she flinched from the touch, his expression turned wistful.

"I guess it's not so easy," he said.

Rowan peered at him; one dark eyebrow arched. "Easy to do what?" she asked, her voice barely more than a breath.

"To trust one another." He moved his hand towards her again. This time she did not pull away as his fingers caressed her face, moving down her cheekbone, curling around her chin.

A strange giddiness overwhelmed her. Color rose in her cheeks as her immortal blood pumped faster in her veins. She moved her own hand towards Azriel, placing it in the hollow between his breast bones, trailing her fingers through the fine dusting of hair on his chest. He did not move away from her touch but curled into it, shifting, so his face was close to hers. She could smell the coppery tang of the serum on his breath, and she struggled to keep her fangs from dropping, from ruining this strange moment. And then his lips were on hers. Rowan's tongue darted out, probing the inside of his mouth.

What am I doing? What the hell am I doing? she thought, but she did not stop. Instead, she let her hand wander down his torso, tracing over his navel. Her fingers moved as if possessed, lower now to the band of his undershorts.

"Is this what you brought me here for?" Azriel asked.

Rowan's hand froze. Her eyes flew open, and she found him staring at her, a lopsided grin on his face, his dark hair falling in disheveled curls across his brow. His hand was cupped around the back of her neck—*Gods, he could so easily snap my neck right now,* she thought.

"I—" She coughed. "I'm sorry. I don't know what came over me. It must have been the aroma of the serum."

Azriel's arm shifted from her neck to the small of her back. He pulled her closer and stared at her. His eyes were smoldering, like liquid flame.

"I think it's more than the serum," he said. His voice was deep and throaty, close to her ear. "I think you're drawn to me, as I am to you. From the moment I first saw you, I felt it. I could have let the change take me. Could have tracked you and killed you in my feral form. But, Rowan, I didn't want to kill you. Couldn't bring myself to do it."

Rowan shuddered. Because Azriel was right. It wasn't the serum she longed for. It was him.

"What is happening?" she asked.

He shook his head. He didn't know either. This was not supposed to happen. He shouldn't be here, and he most certainly shouldn't be attracted to this beautiful, deadly bloodsucker. He changed positions, planting his feet on the floor, scooping Rowan into his arms. She latched her arms around his neck, smelling the wood smoke and forest rain scent of his dark hair.

"Bed?" He breathed the single word as he lifted her.

Rowan raised her hand and pointed towards a door off to the left. She could feel the limp in his step as he carried her into the room and deposited her on the four-poster bed with a wilting canopy. The wood creaked dangerously as he rolled onto his side next to her. His fingers fumbled with her bodysuit, and she laughed as he struggled to unfasten it. Reaching around, she said, "Let me."

Deftly, she unclasped the closures. Azriel's hands followed hers, peeling the fabric away, revealing milky white skin so pale it was nearly translucent. When the garment was removed, he pushed her gently down on the bed. Her naked body unfurled like a flower as she gazed up at him, breathing heavily, lips parted, fangs half extended over her lips.

This is foolishness. Only pain can come from this, Rowan thought. But she did not stop him from lowering his body onto hers and taking her.

Azriel

HER BODY WAS A TEMPLE. It was the moon, flawless, cold, and luminous. Everything about her was deadly, her sharp nails painted red as blood, her fangs skimming just above her full lips, her eyes flashing with passion and threatening violence. Azriel didn't care. If she killed him, he would die in the throes of ecstasy. He would be fine with it.

When at last he was spent, and they were both panting and covered in a sheen of sweat, he rolled off her, twining the midnight waves of her long hair around his fist. He turned his head and looked her dead in the eye.

"I do not care what they say. Nothing that feels this good could be wrong."

Rowan smiled faintly at this, but there was something behind it. *Fear,* Azriel realized. And he understood it. What they were doing here could never be forgiven by their people. Not by the Vampire Elders, and certainly not by the Enforcers.

Azriel started to say something else, but then he noticed she had closed her eyes. Her chest rose and fell in breaths so shallow that they would not sustain a Mortal being. The sleep of the undying. He sat up and untangled the mess they'd made of the sheets, then gently covered himself and Rowan with them. He draped an arm over her body, the inhumanly cool touch of her skin prickling goosebumps on his sweat-drenched skin. Then he, too, fell into a restful slumber.

When Azriel woke, he found night had fallen, and the place on the bed where Rowan had been was empty. He sat up, straining his eyes into the darkness. Getting out of bed, he limped to the door, moving with all the silent prowess of a Wolf that he could muster in his human form. He peeked out into the living area.

Rowan crouched on the floor in the center of the room. In her hands, she clutched the limp corpse of a large rat. Its body looked emptied, a dry husk, as if the lifeblood had been sucked out of it. The shining red smears on her fully extended fangs verified this.

Azriel's stomach muscles clenched. This, he reminded himself, was why his people were charged with destroying them. The virus that had infected them gave them an unquenchable thirst for blood. In the early days after the war, the bloodsuckers had run rampant through Aeturnium and the surrounding lands, bathing it in red to quench their blood lust.

But it had been many years, centuries even, since the Vampires had roved in gangs through the lands. The mortals had found a way to distill blood, voluntarily donated, down to its essence. Serum, they called it. And if that, and few fat rats, were enough to satiate their hunger... Why were they still hunted so mercilessly?

"I did not want you to see this." Rowan's voice rang out and jarred Azriel from his thoughts.

He locked eyes with her. The rat had fallen from her bloody fingers, lying broken on the living room floor. And even now, as she self-consciously licked the last traces of crimson from her lips, she looked beautiful, her small naked body shimmering in the moonlight.

"It's alright," he said. "We all do what we must to survive in this world."

Rowan looked puzzled, like this was not the response she was expected. "Tell me, Lupine, what is it you've done to survive?"

Azriel closed his eyes against the barrage of visions that passed before them. The faces of the dying Vampires he'd strung up to burn in the sunlight or impaled upon his claws.

"Things far worse than this." His voice was hoarse as he gestured at the dead rodent.

Rowan nodded, seeming to understand.

"What will we do when morning comes?" he asked.

Rowan cocked her head at him, the slight birdlike gesture sending a wave of hair spiraling over her shoulder.

"I don't know. But I'm not going to turn you into the Elders."

Azriel nodded and crossed the room, lowering himself to the floor beside her and pulling her into his arms again.

Rowan

The morning dawned cold and dreary. A strong wind blew in from the north, smelling strongly of pine and faintly of snow, a reminder that the lean winter months were coming.

They had spent the remainder of the night wrapped in one another's arms, talking about themselves and their lives. In the end, they learned they weren't so different as they'd thought. Both were bound to their duties, through no choice of their own. Just as Azriel had been groomed since childhood to be an Enforcer, so had Rowan been tasked as a Runner—smuggling serum out of Aeturnium and into Luxorna.

Rowan was rewrapping the bandage around Azriel's thigh when she heard a sound that made her stiffen. A high keening filled the air. It was a mourning cry. The collective lament of the Vampires when one of their own had perished.

Her hands began to shake, and she relinquished her grip on the bandage, leaping to her feet, ignoring the hiss of pain from Azriel.

"Stay here. Keep away from the windows. Let no one in," she ordered, snatching her red cloak up and wrapping herself in it.

"Wait," Azriel called after her, but she didn't turn back to him.

Rowan flew out the door, slamming it behind her. Tearing down the streets towards the city center, the somber lament grew louder with each step. She saw a cluster of Vampires congregating outside the temple. Shoving through the crowd, she made her way towards the towering building.

There was a body lying at the foot of the temple, a red cloak draped over it like a shroud. Blood began to pound in Rowan's temples, white noise rushing in her ears.

"Who is it?" Rowan asked a mourner standing beside her. The woman did not answer, only gazed heavenward, her throat undulating with the mourning song, tears streaming from her eyes.

Rowan stepped forward, out of the crowd, towards the prone figure. No one stopped her as she knelt and drew the red funeral shroud aside, revealing the face of the deceased.

"Lilith," she gasped the name of the ancient Vampire aloud.

How? How could it be? Three thousand years Lilith had survived alone in the Windwood. She couldn't be dead. With shaking hands, Rowan pulled the red cloak back farther, revealing the sucking wound in her chest.

A claw. A claw through her heart. A Lupine Enforcer had killed their Matriarch.

A sob caught in Rowan's throat as she flung the cloak back over the body, covering the gaping hole where her heart had been, concealing the open sightless eyes. Then she turned and fled, forcing her way through the crowd.

She found herself running along the path that led back to her home. Her home, where a wounded Lupine Enforcer awaited her return. When she approached the door, she did not hesitate. She burst through it, her tearful eyes accusing as they fell on Azriel, who was lying on her couch. Rowan glared, eyes gone violet with fury, hurt, and betrayal.

"You killed her!" she screamed, throwing herself at Azriel, raking her sharp nails across his naked chest. He deflected her next blow, leaping to his feet. Hair began to erupt on his body in tufts, but he seemed to be controlling the change. He lunged at Rowan, and she was sure she would feel his claws pierce her own heart. Instead, he only took her by the shoulders and pulled her in close, his arms enveloping her petite frame against the sturdiness of his chest.

"Rowan, I didn't. It wasn't me. Rowan, I swear. It wasn't me."

She pounded on Azriel's chest, her fangs sliding out in her fury. A thin rivulet of blood trickled from her lip where she'd bitten it. She thought about biting him, about sucking every last ounce of his blood out of him as retribution for Lilith. But he pulled her even closer, accepting the flurry of blows as he stroked her hair and whispered into it soothingly, "Rowan, it wasn't me."

"It was one of your kind. One of you dogs," she choked out between sobs.

"It was. I'm sure it was. But it wasn't *me*. I'm not the Pack. You are not the Clan. Rowan, don't you see? We are not them. We don't have to be who they expect us to be."

Their eyes connected, and she stiffened in his embrace. It was true... but it wasn't. Sure, the two of them could change. Could break the cycle of vengeance and retribution. But it would not change the world around them. Their people would still be at war, hell-bent on killing each other.

"This will never work, Azriel," Rowan said, her voice empty of emotion. Still, despite her protest, she collapsed into his embrace, letting him steady her and be her strength.

"We will find a way. We will make this work. Rowan, I know we only just met. I know this sounds crazy. But... you're the only thing I've ever wanted. I saw you in the forest, and I knew—you were meant for me." Azriel drew her face up and kissed her. Her extended fangs sliced into his lower lip, but he continued until she relented, withdrawing her fangs and kissing him back.

Then they both froze, eyes mirroring one another's horror as a new sound mingled with the mourning cries. Long low howls. A hundred at least.

"The Pack," he whispered.

Oh, Goddess, no. Rowan wrenched herself free from Azriel's embrace. She was surprised to see Azriel throw the stolen cloak from Lilith's cabin over his shoulders, but she didn't have time to protest. If he wanted to follow, let him follow. Perhaps the Clan would give him the death that she herself could not mete out.

Lilith was dead. The Pack was here. Her whole world was crumbling.

Azriel

Guilt was an acrid, sour pit burning in Azriel's belly as he ran behind Rowan towards the crumbling gates of Luxorna. His leg screamed in protest with every step, but he did not stop or slow down. He deserved this misery and more. While it had not been his claws that had gauged the old bloodsucker's heart out, he knew whose it had been. Boris. Boris had slain the ancient creature the day before Azriel had come across Rowan in the Windwood.

And Azriel had lied to her about it.

Worse yet, he had a fairly good idea why the Pack of Enforcers had descended upon Luxorna. They were looking for him. He had led the Wolves to the gates of Luxorna, and now there would be blood. A cold sweat broke out on his brow as dread coiled in his belly.

The mourners had already flocked to the gate, a sea of red bodies that parted for Rowan. He shoved through in her wake, careful to keep his own cloak pulled low to cover his face.

As he'd expected, it was Boris standing at the head of a full company of Enforcers. A full company? Did they plan on taking the whole city? They were assembled in a V shape, the Enforcers in the front in their human forms, those in the back mostly feral. In his agitation, Azriel's claws had begun to unsheathe, and fur sprouted in tufts along his arms and on his back.

He had to keep calm. There did not have to be a bloodbath here, if only...

"MURDERERS!" Rowan's voice sliced the air as she burst through the mob of Vampires to stand before the company of Wolves.

Boris frowned down at her, nearly twice her height and brawny. His claws were fully extended, and they were near as long as Rowan's arms.

"We are here under orders from the Overlords," Boris snarled, eyeing Rowan with indifference. "One of our most highly esteemed officers went missing in the night two days hence. We're to put you all to the question until we find him."

Azriel wasn't buying that for a minute. The Overlords would never order an entire company of Enforcers into Luxorna on his account. They *never* trespassed on Luxorna. They had tried before, just once. It had ended in a stalemate, with horrendous losses on both sides. Both Azriel's parents had been killed in that battle. So why were they here now?

"You Wolves killed Lilith," Rowan accused again.

Boris folded his arms across his chest and smirked haughtily at her. "My Wolves didn't kill her. I killed her. And you're next if someone doesn't tell me what happened to Lieutenant Ulv."

Azriel saw Rowan's hand drop to the bandolier around her waist as if in slow motion. The little fool was going to get herself killed. If she pulled a blade on Boris, he would tear her into a thousand pieces. He saw Boris bristle, baring his pointed canines at her with a growl.

Just as Rowan moved to draw her blade, Azriel let the change take him. Claws shot forth where fingers had been, canines elongating. Not full Wolf. He couldn't go full feral. But close. He saw Boris move, knew he was ready to strike, and Azriel leaped from where he had been hidden in the crowd. Around him, the eerie mourning cry of the Vampires became interspersed with screams as they realized there was a Wolf in their midst.

The Pack looked around, trying to determine the source of the commotion, some shifting to prepare for a fight, others remaining sentient and holding back their feral brethren, at least for the moment. Even Boris lost focus on Rowan, his eyes darting to the crowd.

Azriel took advantage of the panic that ensued. He lunged, inserting his body between Rowan and the startled Enforcers. He snarled at Boris, fur bristling on his haunches as they locked eyes.

"Azriel," Boris exclaimed. He blinked twice as if he could not believe his eyes and raised one hand over his head, the signal for the Pack to stand down.

Azriel ignored him, looking to Rowan instead. Her

hand still hovered at her waist, but she had not drawn a blade. He prayed that she wouldn't. To draw that blade would be her death. And it would be on his head.

"Why are you here, Boris?" Azriel growled.

Boris let out a bark of laughter. "Why am I here? I'm here looking for you. The real question is, why are you here, Az? And why are you wearing *that*?"

Azriel had forgotten about the red cloak thrown hastily over his shoulders to conceal himself.

"Azriel," he heard Rowan call from behind him. He twisted his head around. Three fully feral Lupines had slunk away from the rest of the Pack and surrounded her.

"Get away from her," Azriel ordered. He was an officer and an Alpha. They should have obeyed immediately. Instead, they hesitated, looking to Boris for direction. "Boris. Call them off."

Boris glanced at the three Wolves and Rowan, then turned back to Azriel and narrowed his eyes. "Why?"

Azriel's mind raced. Why indeed? What could he say that Boris would understand, that would get through to him? He certainly couldn't tell the truth. Couldn't say he'd fallen for the girl in the red cloak. That would mean certain death for them both. There was no greater taboo than the coupling of a Vampire and a Lupine.

"She's mine. I've been stalking her since that night I disappeared in the Windwood. She wounded me, and I would have my revenge. I've been trying to get close enough for days."

Azriel prayed Boris believed the lie. He turned back

towards Rowan. Her face was pale and expressionless. He could not tell what she was thinking, but he could smell her fear. It was wafting off her in waves, and the feral Enforcers around her were salivating at the scent of it.

"Call them off," Azriel repeated, enunciating each word slowly.

Boris snorted but raised a hand, and the Enforcers melted back into the Pack, snapping at Azriel on the way, angry to have their kill taken from them. "Now tell me why you're really here. I know you, Az. You'd never be fool enough to chase a vamp here." He gestured at the decaying ruins that surrounded them.

"My reasons are my own," Azriel snarled back.

"Azriel, you know you're like a brother to me. But sympathizing with a Vamp—"

"I'm not a Vamp sympathizer. I told you. I was going to kill her."

Boris stared at Azriel for a long moment, his lips set in a grim line, their eyes locked. Azriel could see the doubt warring with his desire to believe his friend and partner.

At last, he sighed and looked away. "Fine. Then kill the girl, if that has been your intent all along, as you say," Boris ordered, folding his arms across his chest.

Azriel's heart almost stopped at the command. He gawked at Boris. This was a man he thought was his closest friend. His partner. They had hunted together, had exchanged jokes around the campfire together, had saved one another's lives on more than one occasion. *Surely* he could not be asking this of him.

Boris prowled closer to Azriel, so close that he could feel his breath on his neck when he whispered, "I am giving you a chance to redeem yourself, brother. I'm not a fool. I can see what is going on here. Kill her now, and I'll never tell a soul about this disgusting tryst of yours."

The blood drained from Azriel's face as he glanced at Rowan. The Wolves had backed off, but they had coalesced around her in a formation that left her with nowhere to run, nowhere to hide. Behind her, a sea of red-cloaked figures keened and fretted, but none seemed prepared to come to her aid. The Vampires would not make the first move.

This was a massacre waiting to happen.

"If I kill her here and now, all those bloodsuckers behind her are going to charge your company. Is that what you want, Boris? To return to the Overlords with news that your whole company has perished? A repeat of the battle that killed our parents? If you return at all, that is. If one of them doesn't rip your throat out and leave nothing but a husk behind."

Boris's eyes roved over the Vampires, and Azriel followed his gaze. There were at least four hundred, all with hands poised on blades, all with sharp white fangs exposed. One move, one false move here and...

Rowan

ROWAN DID NOT SEE who threw the first blade. It came from somewhere behind her, streaking past her close enough that she felt the breeze stir her hair as it passed.

Boris seemed not to see it coming either. If he had, he would have ducked. Instead, the silver blade struck him in the chest with a thump. The Lupine's eyes widened, darted wildly around the crowd as if bewildered, then finally came to rest on Azriel, accusation blazing in them. Azriel's jaw dropped open as his partner slumped and pitched forward, his head smacking the ground with a sickening *crack*. The head wound didn't much matter. Rowan knew how it was with the Lupines. The blade had hit home. Silver, straight through the heart. He was dead before his head struck the earth.

For a moment, there was only stillness, as if neither the Enforcers nor the Vampires could piece together what had just happened. As if both sides thought it some sort of collective hallucination.

Then all hell broke loose.

The Vampires shrieked, their voices raised in a blood-curdling battle cry, and pressed forward as one. The Lupine, without their Alpha commander to rein them in, snarled and shifted into an unruly mass of teeth and fangs. They leaped forward, bounding towards the red-cloaked sea of Vampires.

One charged at Rowan, and she screamed, reaching for her knives, but Azriel was there, snapping at the smaller Wolf, driving it back.

"Run," he growled to Rowan.

She slipped dual knives from their sheaths, and she ran, wielding her knives like a creature possessed, slashing at anything that got in her way, turning her head every so often to make sure Azriel followed. She saw he was limping again. Gods, she had nearly forgotten he was injured. Still, he was pressing steadily forward behind her, his form half-man, half-lupine.

A claw grazed Rowan's cheek, but she dodged before the beast could grab hold of her and stabbed at his gut with his blade. He crumpled to the ground, and she paused, breathing heavily, and brought a hand to her face. Her fingers came away sticky with her own blood.

"Rowan, are you okay?" Azriel stood beside her. She shuddered slightly at the sight of him, covered in tufts of shaggy hair, as he reached a clawed hand out for her.

He seemed to sense her fear at seeing him in this state. "It's still me. I'm still Azriel," he said softly.

A shriek shattered the moment as a waifish, silver-haired Vamp lunged at Azriel, blade held aloft. Rowan twisted, flinging her knife into the air. It landed in the Vamp's chest with a sick sucking sound.

"Traitor," she whispered as she died, and the spell that held Azriel and Rowan frozen in place was broken. They took off together once more, scratching and stabbing their way through the mob until they reached the gates.

They didn't stop there. Blind and mindless with terror, they fled along the High Road until the roar of the battle in the city became a soft din. Skirting off the path, they headed north towards the desolate inhospitable Eliirian mountain range where neither Vampire nor Lupine dared to go. There, it was said, lurked the *real* monsters.

But they had nowhere else to go. They would have to take their chances.

They didn't stop until darkness fell and they reached the foothills. By then, their legs were simply unable to carry them farther. Pausing to rest, they gazed down at the city of Luxorna. Flames blazed from what must have been the city center, and even up here, the air was caustic with smoke.

"Are you alright?" Rowan asked, barely able to formulate words.

Azriel shifted, his tawny fur vanishing, his claws retracting into their sheaths. *It's not so different*, she thought, *from my fangs.*

"I'll live," Azriel said with a wry grin. "But what are we going to do now?"

"We'll go north. Together. We have lived our whole lives calling each other monsters. And look, we are really not so bad. Perhaps the same is true of the demons in Eliirian."

THE END

Soul of the Ocean

Lana

⸎

I WAS BORN Lana of the Fae Beneath the Waves, one of Lord Marin's seven daughters. Heir to oyster pearls and gold plundered from the ships we sank with our sweet songs. I stood to inherit a trove of treasure when I came of age and wed. The eldest of the Lord's daughters, I would be betrothed to a Lordling from the Court of Sky, or Dreams, perhaps. I would want for nothing. The lesser Water Faerie, the Kelpies and the Gwragedd Annwn, all the Asais, would be at my beck and call to serve my every need and whim.

But that wasn't enough for me. I wanted more. Inside me brewed a deep, crippling fear of the day I would dissolve into sea foam on a breaker and simply cease to be. And I could trace this obsession with the afterlife back to one day in my Auntie Ula's cave.

Ula was my father's eldest sister, a Sea Fae like all of us but different. Her face was strikingly beautiful, smooth as abalone and pearlescent, but from the crown of her head sprouted writhing sea snakes of turquoise and gold who hissed on command. Her waist was narrow, her hips wide, tapering to a fishtail, but from it sprang long tentacles. Most feared Ula and whispered that she practiced the old magic, the blood magic, and had been corrupted by it.

Even my sisters shied from Ula, but not me. As a child, I would drift at her fins, enraptured by her stories. A teller of tales, a weaver of words, the wielder of dark, powerful magic. I adored Ula. And it was from her that I first learned of yet another sort of magic. The secret magic that only mortals possessed. Their immortal souls.

"Sorrow is the cross that the mortals must bear in life," Ula said as my sisters and I crowded around the foot of her seat, hewn from purple coral deep within her sea cave. "Their life in this world is but a blink of a Fae's eye. They toil in the fields until their bodies fail them. They watch the light go out in the eyes of their friends and lovers. Mortal mothers grieve for children lost to the vapors of pestilence, then they too succumb to sorrow and old age. Ashes to ashes, dust to dust, as they say."

A single pearlescent tear leaked from my eye as Ula spoke and began a slow glide down one cheek, mingling with the saltwater.

"Lana's crying," my sister Lalia crowed, pointing and laughing at me. Of course, my other five sisters all joined in mocking my tears until Ula held up a hand to silence their jibes. No one dared defy my Auntie, so they quickly went quiet.

Ula looked at me, her lips pressing into a frown.

Then she reached out with a tentacled arm and brushed my tears away. "Lana, child, why is it that you weep?"

I sniffed back a sob and replied, "Because it is so sad. All those struggles, all that heartache, and for what? Just the briefest moment in the sun? They lose everything, and then they just die." I cried even harder as I choked out the words.

Ula smoothed my scarlet hair back from my brow and soothed me with whispered words. "Shhh, hush, child. There is no need for this blubbering. Though we Fae may live many hundreds, even thousands, of human lives, they have something to look forward to which we, alas, do not."

I blinked back my tears and gazed up at my aunt, who stared at me with a knowing look in her ancient, iridescent eyes. "What do you mean?" I asked her.

"Mortals have an immortal soul," she whispered so softly that my sisters could not hear. As if it were a secret for only me to know.

I furrowed my brow, unfamiliar with the term. "What is a soul?" I asked.

Ula cocked her head as if considering her words. "It is... a spark, which resides in the heart of each mortal being. When they slip from the bondage of their frail earthly bodies, their souls carry on, for eternity, in the realm beyond."

I considered this, then asked, "Do we not get to venture to the world beyond?"

Ula shook her head. "We are Sea Fae. We return to the sea when our time here is done. Our spirits go to the

Void, and our bodies become the froth on the waves. So it has always been. The mortals believe we are the immortal ones, when in fact it is them."

This did not sit right to me, and I spoke out in protest. "And if I do not wish to go quietly into nothingness? Can I not have a soul too?"

Ula's lip flattened into a thin line. "No, but we are blessed with innumerable years of life, beyond even the imaginings of a mortal. Do not fret, child. Put the Void from your mind. It will be many long centuries before it will call to you. Go now, Lana, and play with your sisters." She ushered me off, breaking the spell of her gaze that held me in thrall.

I glanced around. My sisters had indeed dispersed. I caught sight of them playing with a pod of dolphins together. I did not want to play with them. I longed to know more about the mortals and their souls, but I dared not press my aunt for further details. At least not right away.

I went off to join my siblings, racing skates and porpoise through the jewel-toned reefs we called home. But the speck of sand that would become my obsession was already set, a pearl of curiosity growing in the shell of my young mind.

* * *

I was an incorrigible child. I badgered everyone I knew relentlessly for months after that day to learn more. Would I truly one day simply cease to be and meld into the salty waters of the sea? The idea of nothingness terrified me. Why were humans spared this fate, but we Fae were not? Were we not, after all, the more powerful race? Blessed with magic and strength far greater than the fragile, powerless humans? Did we not also deserve immortality? And what was this world beyond like? Was it possible it could be more perfect than our shining Court beneath the sea?

I asked all these questions and more of my father, and of every elder Fae, until one day Lord Marin, at his wit's end, ordered me into his throne room.

"Lana," he began, perched atop his gleaming throne of polished sea glass, trident in hand. His brow was creased, his lips set in a stern scowl. "I will not have you harrying half the kingdom with your relentless questions about *mortals.*" He said the last word with bitter disdain.

"But father—" I began.

Lord Marin swirled out of his throne, his powerful tail churning the water into rapidly spinning eddies. "Do not interrupt me, girl. Listen, and listen well. I do not like this interest you've taken in those pathetic creatures who live above the waves. But since none of us will get a moment's peace, I will grant you a boon if you promise that will be the end of it.

"On the day you come of age, I will let you go the surface and call out to a mortal ship, sinking it with your voice. I'm quite sure once you see how pathetic and weak-willed these mortal sailors are, that will be the end of your unbecoming interest in them."

I considered this for a moment. My coming of age was a long way off. I did not want to wait so long. But I could sense that my father would be unyielding. I could accept this offer or not, but there would be no brokering a better deal. So I bowed my head in acquiescence.

"As you wish, Father. I'll stay my tongue. Not another word until I come of age."

Of course, I did not know how to sink a ship with my voice. But I knew someone who did. I was Ula's favorite niece. I knew she would never deny me my deepest desire. And so, I waited.

Lana

IT WAS many centuries in the markings of mankind before the topic of mortals was broached again in the Court of Sea. A Sea Fae's childhood is long and full of distractions. Most would have forgotten Ula's tales and my father's promise, letting them drift away like a stream of bubbles, a youthful fancy on a passing current, forgotten once it has swept by.

But not me.

I clung to my obsession with all the tenacity of a shark with prey seized in its sharp teeth. I heeded my vow to my father and did not utter a word until the time was right, but in my mind, I wandered the sandy shores of the humans, seeking a way to claim one of their souls for my own.

Then, at last, the day of my coming of age arrived. I was out of my silvery clamshell bed before the first rays of the sunrise could trickle down to the watery depths of our halls. I had carefully considered my plan and knew it hinged on one thing: getting Auntie Ula to agree to sink a ship for me. I knew nothing of mortals, neither where to find them nor what to do when I did. But Ula... Ula knew it all.

And so I swam along through the familiar patches of coral and the gardens teeming with anemones of every shape and hue until I approached Ula's sea caves.

I never understood why my aunt chose to spend her days and nights in the impenetrable darkness of the sea caves, only that once long ago, she and my father had quarreled, and now she chose to live alone in this dark place.

Soon, I would learn about the old magic, the dark magic, that Ula practiced. Stolen spells from another people and another time. Magic that my father did not wish to harbor within his walls.

That morning, though, I was innocent to such knowledge and brimming with excitement when I approached before the crack of dawn. "Aunt Ula! Do you know what today is?" I cried enthusiastically as I swished around the mouth of her cave.

"I know it is very early in the morning, whatever day it is," came her grumble from within the dark recesses. "What do you want, Lana?"

"My father promised me long ago that on the day I come of age, you would bring me to the surface and wreck a ship for me, that I might see these mortals you tell tales of with my own eyes."

It was a lie. Lord Marin had promised no such thing.

But he was the Sea Lord, and Ula would be bound to respect his command.

Ula propelled herself from the depths of the cave to stand before me, her sea snakes snapping their fangs. "Marin promised you that *I* would do this, did he? Well, the Lord of Sea does not command Ula and never has. That is why I live here, alone. He's in no position to make promises on my behalf."

I gasped at the blasphemy my aunt dared speak. "He is the Lord of the Court of Sea. All are subject to his rule. His word is law. If you do not bring me to the surface, I'll... well, I'll..."

"You'll what?" she challenged.

Heat rose in my cheeks, and tears burned behind my eyes. Surely Ula knew how long I had waited for this day, how it was my heart's one desire. How could she be so cruel? And to deny my father's command? That was unthinkable!

"I'll have you turned in for treason, and I'll sink a ship myself. You're a rotten old sea witch. A washed-up, powerless hag, drunk on blood magic, just as everyone in the palace claims."

The sea snakes in Ula's writhed and hissed at the venomous words I spat. Her face turned vivid purple, and I took a step back, sure she was going to slap me. Instead, she lashed out with a tentacle, wrapping it around my wrist, dragging me towards the cave's mouth.

"You want to sink a ship, do you? Think I'm powerless? Well then, come, Lana. We shall sink a whole fleet if that's what you want," she growled. Then, in a low voice, she went on. "Do not think I'm doing this because your father ordered it, Princess. Oh, I recognized that glint in your eyes every time I told a tale about the mortals. What is it you want from them, Lana? What is it you think you can gain?"

I wasn't sure what to say. I couldn't very well tell the truth. Ula would likely outright call off the whole endeavor and possibly inform my father if I told her I longed to claim a human soul for my own. Then I would be barred from the surface for a very long time. Most likely until my father and Ula both dissolved into seafoam themselves.

"I'm just curious," I lied again, not meeting Ula's eyes.

My aunt did not look convinced by my explanation, but she muttered something inaudible under her breath and released my wrist.

"I shall take you on this fool's errand and be done with it once and for all."

Ula used her powerful tail and tentacles to power up towards the surface, and I followed behind, struggling to keep up. For the first time, I witnessed the radiance of light blooming around us as we broke the surface, water droplets dancing like shattered crystals in the sun. I look around, dazzled. I heard a strange sound and turned my head to see a swarm of white and gray birds. They dipped below the surface of the waves then emerged, small fishes with shimmering scales clutched in their beaks.

"Gulls. They are pests. Don't feed them, or we'll

never be rid of them," Ula scoffed, following my eyes. "Come, let's have done with this."

We swam towards a large rock outcropping jutting above the surface of the waves some distance from the shore. I couldn't take my eyes off the beach, the way the sand twinkled like millions of unimaginably tiny white gems in the brilliant brightness. The sun caressed my skin with a warmth unknown to me, and the breeze tugged my hair, like gentle fingers toying with the tendrils, pushing them back away from my face.

Excitement pulsed through me. At last, the chance to see humans, the mythical creatures of Ula's tales, with my own eyes. "When will they come?" I asked, gaze shifting from the wide swathe of beach to the great expanse of the open ocean.

"Soon," Ula growled.

It was a long wait, and I grew drowsy in the warmth of the sun. My eyes had dropped closed when I felt the weight of Ula's tentacle upon my shoulders.

"Look, there." She pointed, and I bolted upright, squinting into the distance. All I saw was a black and white speck on the horizon.

"Is that a ship? It's so tiny!"

"Fool," Ula muttered. Then she raised a tentacle and began to utter words in a language that was only vaguely familiar to me. The Old Tongue, a Magic long ago pilfered from the Elves that only the oldest and most powerful Fae still knew.

As the ship approached, it began to change direction, moving away from the open sea and towards the rocky shore where Ula and I lay in wait. Drawing nearer, the great white sails came into view and the broad bow with a chiseled figurehead of a woman's face. Behind the ship, a massive cloud unfurled, inky black on the horizon, blotting out the sun. I watched with wide eyes as the forms of men, small as ants in the distance, scurried around the decks, hauling ropes and shouting words I could not make out. Desperate cries riding the storm's winds.

There was a tremendous crash of thunder, and a lightning bolt severed the sky, a forked pillar streaking down, aimed directly at the ship. Sparks flew, and fire blossomed on the ship's deck. I gasped and covered my mouth.

I turned to Ula and exclaimed, "They will die!"

Ula's face was grim. She did not appear to take any great joy in this, but neither did she seem particularly distraught. "Indeed. What did you think would happen when their ship sank?"

Whatever I had expected, it certainly was not this. I could not steal a soul from a dead man. I knew that much. And all these mortals would surely drown in Ula's storm.

As the flaming ship drew near, I could make out the forms and faces of the men more clearly. They rushed desperately around the deck, hauling buckets of water and attempting to staunch the flames, but they only grew higher and more ravenous. Soon, sailors were throwing themselves overboard to escape the inferno. As I watched, one man, young with hair the color of the distant sandy beach and horrified eyes, climbed onto the ship's prow.

The mortal was beautiful. He stood there like a deity, a lord of sea and sky, illuminated by the silver forked sky, like a star poised to explode. He raised his arms up above his head, and then he dove, disappearing beneath the waves.

"No!" As his body submerged, I sprang from the rocky outcropping into the wildly churning sea.

"Lana!" Ula's voice carried over the roar of the whipping winds, but I ignored her, plunging beneath the surface. The currents were strong, but they were no match for my prowess. I was the daughter of a Fae lord, and the waves bent to my command. I beat my powerful tail, propelling towards the capsized ship through the water, towards *him*.

I don't know what drew me to him, of all the sailors aboard that sinking vessel. I had no idea he was a prince amongst men. Perhaps it just seemed a waste that a creature so young and beautiful should perish from this world, immortal soul or not. Surely there was more in this world he'd like to experience before his mortal life was snuffed out.

Or maybe it was destiny. The cruel hand of the Goddess at work.

Whatever the source of the call, I heeded it, desperately searching the water. Flotsam floated by, whisked away by the powerful current of Ula's magic. Broken boards from the shattered ship and tangles of dark kelp. Then, at last, a hand, pale and sinking fast. I sped towards it, grasped it, and hauled the mortal to the surface. He took three great, gasping breaths, then fell unconscious.

He was a tall man, broad-shouldered, with a powerful physique. Carrying him to the shore was no easy task, even with my powerful tail and sway over the waves. Yet somehow, I made it.

For the first time, sand kissed my skin. Rough, sloughing away the delicate scales of my tail, but I ignored the sting and placed my hand upon the mortal's chest. I felt it then. Not just his heart beating steadily or the rise and fall of his chest with each labored breath. I felt his soul. Primal, fragile. Indescribable. I tried to grasp it, to pull it to me, but it was like trying to cling to a beam of light. I could feel its flow on the surface, but the deeper it went, the more elusive it became.

"Lana!" Ula's voice shattered my reverie. I looked back over my shoulder at her. She stood at the water's edge, her tentacled arms reaching out for me, drawing me back to the sea. My home. Where I belonged.

When I looked back at the man, his eyes were wide open. I had never seen a forest, only heard tales of them from Ula's lips. "Green," she had said, "not green like seagrass or coral. Green like nothing beneath the waves. Deeper, earthier. Green like you've never seen before."

And it was all true. His eyes were the first forest I had ever seen. Later, I would come to see others. Forests full of trees old and young, in winter, spring, summer, and fall. But none would ever compare to the one I first discovered in his eyes.

"You saved me." His voice was hoarse from the swallowed saltwater but rich and deep. In it, I heard the song I craved again. The melody of his soul.

A flare of panic surged in my chest. He was not supposed to wake up, not supposed to see me. If the Sea Lord ever found out... I shifted, backing away, towards the waves and Ula, sand still abrading my delicate flesh. The salt spray of the breakers slicked my iridescent tail, but before I could flee, he grabbed me by the wrist.

"Who are you?"

"Lana," I told him in the Sea Fae tongue, the siren's song. Then I wrenched free, diving into the breakers disappearing into the watery Realms no mortal could ever roam.

It could have ended there. It should have ended there. But it did not.

Alaric

THE WIND BLEW in from the west, light as a lover's breath upon the nape of my neck. Today, the water was calm, lapping against the shore with a gentleness that made it difficult to believe that just days ago, a storm of monumental proportions, capable of sinking my flagship, had laid siege to this shore.

It was no natural storm. With the first gust of the wind, I knew that. Foul magic mounted the waves and lashed out from the sky. My father had told me of the gales of the Undine, the Sea Fae, but I'd thought them nothing more than a tired old man's ramblings, grand embellishment he'd added to make his tales more exciting. After all, we were seafaring folk, the strength of our fleet our greatest asset. Why would an aging king with a shattered leg, a scattered mind, and a weak constitution not embellish the escapades of his youth if it would better his appearance in the eyes of his people?

Whether my father had faced the Undine himself too

or simply pilfered a story that wormed into his ear in some port city tavern, I would never know. The old man had lost his mind almost entirely by the time I experienced my brush with magic and death. But I knew what I had seen.

Not just the sudden nature and unholy violence of the waves... but her. Lana. Magic was real. The Sea Fae were out there, and I owed one of them my life. I wanted to repay her with my heart, for she was the most beautiful creature I had ever seen. A Sea Fae with hair of scarlet and gold, her eyes the pale blue-gray of winter's ice-capped swells.

But this beauty was also likely responsible for the gale in the first place. Her, or one like her. Twenty-nine good men lost their lives when my Mirabelle went down. Seasoned sailors who didn't deserve to come to such an end. Still, though I knew she was to blame for the tragedy, every day since his ship sank, I walked this stretch of beach. Hoping to catch a glimpse of her.

"You're out here looking for trouble, Alaric. It's a bad business, getting mixed up with the Fae. But here you are, seeking them out."

I stopped walking and turned to face my brother. Roland was shorter than me, all dark where I was light, with a slightly hooked nose and fine lines crinkling the edges of his eyes, though he was younger than me. Roland worried, often and about everything. It took a toll.

I gave him a faint smile and slapped him on the back.

"You worry too much, Roland. I'm just going for a walk."

Roland clicked his tongue. "Along the same stretch of beach you've been walking for days? A stretch of beach you never set foot on before you saw *her*?"

Turning away from him, I scanned the horizon. Far off, something stirred the surface, and my heart beat a little faster, eyes widening – but no. Only a school of dolphins, slicing silver across the azure surface of the cold, deep water. For a moment, I wondered – If I were to throw myself in, give myself over to the sea's fury, would she find me and save me once again?

"You see? There it is, that look. I recognize it, brother. Funny, I never thought you were the sort to fall in love. You spurned all the matches father and his counselors tried to make for you. But here you are with that dumbstruck look on your face, seeking the one woman in the world you ought to run far, far away from."

He spoke the truth, but I was ashamed to admit it. Some did not believe in the Fae. Until my brush with Lana, I was among them. My brother never was. Roland had taken the tales of the Fae as gospel since he was a boy. Never doubting a word of what I had always believed to be fantasy. Another bogeyman for him to worry about, I had thought. But I was wrong. They were real, and I was in love with one of them.

"Come, brother. We've yet another feast full of suitors this evening," I said with a smile that he did not return.

"I only hope one catches your eye and sways you from this folly," was his dour reply.

* * *

The feast that night was quite the affair. Braziers lit the grand hall, and a fire roared in the hearth, keeping the drafts at bay. Even in summer, there was an evening chill in these northern lands. The long, narrow table was set with the finest silver and china. My father sat at the head, looking frail and gaunt in his purple robes. His handlers, the Vizier and the Master at Arms, flanked him on either side, prepared to sweep him from the room should any inkling of his madness rear its ugly head.

As was the custom, the men were seated first. Once all were in place, the procession of prospective suitors filed into the room. Three, this time, from other great Kingdoms and powerful families. I had tired of this charade long ago, but I put on my practiced fake smile as always. My father, or his counselors, more accurately, wanted me to marry to produce an heir. But I refused to marry a woman I did not love. I had seen the way my parents forced union had worn on them both – my mother, dead before her time, my father, driven mad with guilt, a great man once, now a shriveled husk. I would not follow in their footsteps.

The Vizier rose. "My King Aerion, my Prince Alaric" —he bowed to them both—"I give you Lady Meadow of Waverly." The doors in the rear of the great hall creaked open, and the first girl stepped through. Her head was bowed demurely as she made her way towards the dais in the center of the room. A hiss of "stand up straight" came from the girl's father seated at a table off to the left. But it didn't matter. She was too young and skinny for my taste, with hair the color of straw and eyes of cornflower blue. Fair enough, but frail-looking and shy. Not what I sought in a queen.

As she took her seat, the Vizier's voice filled the room once more, and the second girl appeared at the back of the hall. "Lady Emilicity of Sur." This one was beautiful, to be sure, but there was a coldness about her. Her face was pressed into a sour pucker as if she'd caught a whiff of bad cheese. I did not want an unpleasant harpy for a wife, so I cut my eyes to the Vizier as if to say, 'Get on with this charade.'

"And, finally, Lady Margaery of Trystane."

Bored, I glanced at the final girl, expecting to be underwhelmed. Yet... this one caught my eye. Tall and slender with red hair, though not so red as Lana's. More like a strawberry blonde. She wore a faint smile and held her head high as if the room were hers to command.

"A true queen, this one," Roland, seated beside me, leaned in and whispered.

My brother was right, and for a moment, all thoughts of Lana flew from my mind. I stood, lifted my chalice, and chimed my knife against it three times. The crowd's din receded to a hushed silence.

"Good Lords and Ladies, it is time"—I turned to face the minstrels arranged in the back of the room—"for a dance."

I stepped away from the table and proceeded towards the dais where the three princesses sat. All three girls watched, wide-eyed. Disappointment flickered on Emilicity's face and relief on Meadow's as I approached Margaery and extended my hand towards her.

"My lady," I said, leaning in close to her, "may I have this dance?"

A smile blossomed across her face, her cheeks flushing slightly as she rose, accepted my invitation, and stepped down from the dais. We walked hand-in-hand to the center of the great hall. Though all eyes in the room were upon us, Lady Margaery did not shy from their gazes. She stood across from me, and together we raised our hands. Around us, other couples joined as the music began. The melody of the pipes and lyres started slow. Margaery stepped into me, and I lowered one hand onto her shoulder. She spun, the picture of elegance, as if she had been born to grace a dance floor, then stepped away. A coy smile flirted with her lips when she stepped forward again, and my hand wrapped around her waist, pulling her close.

We were joined for this part of the song, moving in perfect harmony with the waltz. I leaned towards her, flaring my nostrils as the scent of her hair – a summer grove, honeysuckle, citrus, something I couldn't put my finger on.

"So, what is Trystane like, my Lady?" I whispered.

She turned her head just so, and our eyes met again. My heart beat faster in my chest. "Very different from here, my Prince. Full of lush fields, groves of olives and persimmons, warm all year round."

My face fell. Perhaps, I thought, Lady Margaery wouldn't like it here. But she stifled that fear with a gentle squeeze of her hand in mine. "But not nearly so beautiful as your kingdom. Nazure is so wild and untamed. Your sea rages. Your mountains claw at the sky. This land is so full of life... of passion."

She moistened her lips with her pink tongue, and my resolve wavered. I wanted to whisk her from this hall. To show her right then and there how wild Nazure and its men truly were.

But that would not be princely of me. So, instead, I gave her a roguish smile and brought her hand to my lips, tendering it with a kiss as the final notes of the waltz played, then walked her back to her place upon the dais. We paused there, and I bowed deeply, then said, "I hope you would humor me and let me take you on a short tour of the countryside on the morrow."

Her face lit up like the sun itself had burst through the walls of the castle to shine upon her. "I should like that very much, Prince Alaric."

Lana

BACK BENEATH THE WAVES, the tides ebbed and flowed as they always had. I tried to return to my life as it was before, but I couldn't get the surface - and the sailor - from my mind. Dreams of him swirled behind my closed eyelids. I got lost in the verdant jungle of his eyes, night after night. I felt the pulsing beat of his soul, heard the sweet swan song of it, more seductive than any verse from a siren's lips.

Ula had been furious with me for revealing myself to the man, and for many days I stayed away from her, fearing her reprisals. But finally, I could stand it no more. I returned to my aunt's cave and stood before her.

"I wish to go back," I announced.

Ula looked up from the concoction she had been mixing, snorted, and rolled her eyes. "Go, then. You don't need my help. Swim to the surface, child. Sink a ship, bring more wealth to your father's kingdom and—"

I glowered at her and interrupted with, "I don't want to sink a ship. I want to walk with the mortals, learn from them. Become one of them. I want a soul." I did not add *I want to make love to the mortal prince* to the litany of my desires, though the thought flitted through my head like a bit of driftwood caught up in the tide.

Ula sighed in exasperation, the snakes of her hair hissing their frustration along with her. "You cannot be what you are not. You cannot have what is not yours to possess, Lana."

My lips pressed into a frown, and I narrowed my eyes at her. "There must be a way. I know you know the Old Magic, the Blood Magic. Tell me how. I'll do anything."

"Even if there were a way, I would not do it. All magic comes at a cost," Ula snapped at me. "Blood magic, most of all. And the cost for this is far too great. For anyone, but especially for you, a spoiled little princess who has always had her every whim catered to. Not this time, Lana."

The words 'Blood Magic' rang in my ears. The forbidden powers that had gotten Ula barred from my father's palace, ostracized in a court where she should be royalty. Did I dare meddle with such ancient forces?

Because I was a young fool, I did. "I will tell my father you taught me Blood Magic behind his back if you don't do it," I threatened. "And I will learn it. If not from you, from someone else. I will walk with mortals or go to the Void trying."

Ula set down the vials she had been sorting and stared at me. "Do not threaten me, girl."

I held my ground, defiant. "I seek immortality at any cost. Let me walk amongst the mortals, or I swear to the Old Gods of Blood and Black Magic—"

"What do you know of the Old Gods?" Ula was on me faster than one of her conjured lightning bolts, her tentacle gripping my arm. "You think this is a game? You think the Old Gods do not watch over you even now, witnesses to your folly? This is your *last* chance to put this foolishness aside and leave my caves, Lana. Threaten me again, and I shall grant your wish, and you will see what the Old Gods do to those who mock them."

The indigo orbs of Ula's eyes shifted to onyx, and the water around us seemed to grow colder. I shivered, goosebumps pricking my skin. Just as she had when we had gone above to sink the ship, Ula seemed to morph from my kindly old aunt into something powerful. Something terrible.

And I knew, at that moment, she was capable of doing it. And she would if I just pushed once more. "I swear on the Old Gods and on the Goddesses, I will tell him, Ula," I growled through a clenched jaw, trying to conceal the chattering of my teeth as the sea grew colder still.

She did not look angry when she turned around. She looked resigned, almost... calculating.

"There is only one way for a Fae to gain an immortal soul." She drew the words out then paused.

"How? Tell me, and I will do it. Anything."

"It will be painful. No, not painful. Excruciating."

Her eyes burned into mine, chips of dark onyx with crimson. "True love's kiss."

I blinked. For what could be so terrible about a simple kiss? Seeing my confusion, Ula went on.

"But not just any kiss. A kiss that steals the breath of your lover. A kiss that compels them to sacrifice their soul. And there are... stipulations... that come with living as a mortal."

I did not ask her what the stipulations were. Perhaps I was afraid to know. Afraid that if I learned what horrors were in store, I would not be as brave as I thought.

"One cycle of the moon, the pale Goddess who watches over the mortals in the sky. That is all the time you will have. Should you fail, you cannot return to the Sea Court. Do you understand? You are forsaking your Fae existence for a shot in the dark, a chance, however slim it may be, at securing immortality. If you fail... you go to the Void."

Immortality. That word again. When the bones of my father, my sisters, even Ula herself and her Black Magic were washed away with the tide... I would still exist if I could only claim a soul.

"I understand."

But Ula wasn't done yet. "And there will be a sacrifice."

I furrowed my brow. "What sort of sacrifice?"

"I cannot say, child. Magic takes what it will. The Old Gods will take their fee in the manner they choose."

But what did I have to lose? Without a soul, I was

doomed to the Void. But with one... *immortality*. And the love of a prince.

"Do it," I whispered. "Make me a mortal girl."

Ula gave me a long look, then sighed deeply. "As you wish, child."

Unhurried, she began selecting items from her driftwood shelves. The gray, leathery skin of a manta, bulging eyes from an unknown fish, a blue-green viscous fluid in a gold-stoppered bottle. She added all of these to a single vial capped with a death's-head.

"One cycle of the moon, Lana," Ula whispered as she turned to me, holding the bottle aloft. "This will require a Geis," she went on, "of blood."

I gritted my teeth. A Geis. A magic bond sealed in blood. There would be no escaping my fate when it came down to it. I would succeed, or I would be Unmade. Seafoam on the waves. So it was, with a Blood Geis.

Swallowing hard, I nodded to Ula. "I understand."

Ula's gaze cut me to the bone, eyes drilling down into my very core.. I do not know what she saw there, but she floated closer to me. I extended my hand to accept the vial from her. Her ice-cold fingers clamped over mine as she passed me the concoction.

"Hold it steady. Do not spill it." Then she took my free hand and raised it up. From the table, she picked up a long silver blade with a skull engraved on the pommel. Before I had time to react, she slashed my wrist, then her own, pressed them together, and let our mingled blood flow into the open mouth of the vial.

"Drink it down, Lana. Then swim to the surface, fast

as you can. It will not be long before the effects are felt. If you are caught beneath the waves when the change happens, all is lost."

She pulled away from me, our blue blood swirling in the water around us as I brought the concoction to my lips. The noxious fumes made me gag, bile rising up in the back of my throat and threatening to choke me. Still, I drank deeply and swallowed it down until not a drop remained.

Ula's shove came from behind. "Go, you fool of a girl," she hissed. Her tentacle tightened around my waist, and she hurled me from her cave. "Swim to the surface or die!"

And so I did.

Beating my tail, I shot up towards the glittering surface, where the sunlight scattered like diamonds, falling in bright pockets. Then I felt it. The burning agony in my chest, fire in my lungs. I gasped but only managed to swallow a mouthful of water that choked me. Air, of course, I needed air. I tried to beat my tail, but suddenly it felt strange, leaden and heavy, uncoordinated. My vision darkened around the edges as my body, now that of a mortal, starved for oxygen.

In the end, I could do nothing but relinquish myself to the power of the waves. Whether through luck or Ula's magic, the current carried me up. My helpless body was caught by an enormous, rolling breaker as I broke the surface. I was terrified it would swallow me, dragging me back down to the depths of the sea to meet my demise.

Instead, it lifted me, carrying me aloft until it crashed ashore.

The force of the collision of the wave against the beach knocked the air I'd so desperately fought for from my lungs. I slammed hard into the sand, and it scraped my flesh, forced its way into my mouth along with seawater.

And then the wave receded. I was left lying there, a beached thing, bruised, gasping for oxygen through bloody lips. I shivered, staring up at a thick wall of gray clouds, no sunlight to warm me in this strange new body I had so longed for.

After a time, when my breath regained a steadiness, I tried to rise. An agony unlike any I'd ever felt lanced through me. I stared at my outstretched legs, my feet, and the tiny toes. When I flexed them, the pain was there again. A scream welled inside me, but no sound emerged when I opened my mouth. Was it the swallowed seawater?

No. Ula's warning rushed back. "The Gods will choose their fee."

They had stolen my tail and my siren song.

Alaric

MY COURTSHIP WITH MARGAERY ENSUED, and my brush with Lana and the Fae became only a flickering memory in the back of my mind. We toured my kingdom for weeks, visiting fishing villages where the smallfolk quickly grew to love her grace and sweetness, much as I did.

Then, one day, I brought Margaery to the Pine Barrens, the wide swathe of towering black jack oaks, red pines, and white cedars that surrounded my castle on three sides. We walked arm and arm, our footfalls soft on the hummus of the forest floor as the birds and insects sang their accompaniment to our courtship.

A rush of gold caught my eye. I tugged at Margaery's arms, drew a finger to my lips, and pointed. There, just ahead in the small clearing, stood a red-tailed fox. It stood motionless, whiskers twitching as it caught our scent. The tiny gasp and smile of wonder that broached Margaery's face as she caught sight of it made my heart sing. After a moment, the fox was gone, scurrying off into the brush.

"Oh, what a beautiful creature!" Margaery exclaimed.

I chuckled. "Have you no foxes in Trystane?"

She shook her head, strawberry curls bouncing, letting off another waft of her sweet perfume. "No, my Lord. Your forest is so very different from our fields and valleys. So beautiful and full of life."

When she turned away from where the fox had stood to look up at me, her pink lips were parted, her cheeks flushed pink from the exertion of our walk. I brought a hand to her chin, cupping it and leaning down, so her face was close to mine. Smelling the mint of her shallow breaths and the citrus in her hair, I wrapped my arm around her waist, pulling her closer.

"Margaery," I whispered, my voice thick with desire, "I want you to see my whole world. I want you in it, a part of it. Every day for the rest of my life."

I leaned in, pressing my lips against hers. They were softer than velvet, and when her tongue darted into my lips, she tasted sweeter than any fruit I'd ever bitten.

"I've had enough view of the trees," she said, pulling away so abruptly that it brought a burst of laughter to my lips. "Perhaps there's a good view of the entire forest you'd like to show me?"

I immediately thought of the cliffside.

"Follow me," I said, mounting my horse and she following suit. "I know a place with a great view. Just... don't race."

"Afraid my horse can outrun yours?"

"Just trust me," I said. "Horses are surefooted, but that can change—"

"Is it that path ahead?" she asked.

"Well, yes. But—"

She took off, looking back with the ornery grin of someone who doesn't know any better.

"Hey, wait!"

The path narrowed to a seldom walked trail, and then the pines got thicker and thicker.

"Stop! The cliffs come sooner than you'd think," I called after her as the trees became less dense. I knew it wasn't far until the clearing before the cliffside.

The worst thoughts of Margaery losing her life in my company made me throw all caution to the wind, and I spurred my horse on until I caught up.

"Stop!"

She pulled the reins of her horse, and I did the same. Both were a few strides from open air, overlooking a three hundred-foot drop where the firs looked closer to grass than trees.

"Are you crazy?" I demanded.

"No," she said. "Just eager to know I'm not marrying a coward."

I wanted to scold her, but I couldn't help but smile as she broke out in laughter.

I tried to hold onto any rage, but her smile reminded me why I was struck with her in the first place. Her laughter was momentarily stifled by her breath, which resulted in a nasal snort, which finally broke the dam of my lungs, and my relieved chuckling met hers.

"You were right, though," Margaery said. "It's the perfect spot."

"For what?" I asked.

"To rest my thighs, of course," she said. "I'm laughing, but don't think I wasn't terrified. I was holding onto my saddle with all the strength my body could muster."

Margaery squatted in her gown a few times, knowing it was just the two of us, and any propriety could be overlooked in the relative privacy of the Barrens. I never saw so much bare flesh on a woman my own age.

My heart quickened again, and I walked my horse back to the clearing and tied him up. Margaery wasn't far behind.

"You thought I was a coward?" I asked.

"No," she said. "But I figured if I had to be put to the test against so many other suitors, you could do the same."

A stream was running nearby, and I couldn't help but think of the water heading toward the rivers and into the sea. The same sea my beautiful Lana had saved me from then disappeared back into.

Even though I was doing my duty to entertain the idea of courtship and marriage, I couldn't shake the hope that Lana was waiting for my return.

If she could see me now, I thought. *God, I hope heartbroken women of the sea don't turn to foam like in the old tales.*

I shook my head to clear it, my thoughts returning to

Margaery when she wrapped her arms around my chest from behind.

Her chin rested on my shoulder, and I felt the swell of her chest against my back. It was a warmth I had never known.

"Can you make a fire?" she asked. "Or is that something for servants and squires?"

I smiled and turned toward her.

"I'll have you know, princes in the land of Nazure are self-reliant," I said. "Everyone that can swing an axe can build a fire and sail a ship."

I smelled her scent again. The summer grove, the honeysuckle, and the citrus underneath her other aroma.

"Your majesty?" Margaery asked. "You've been quiet since we got here. Something amiss? Surely my little stunt didn't anger you. I promise I'm an accomplished rider."

Feigning affection, I drew her closer. "No. Just royal responsibilities weighing on my mind. Nothing new."

She smirked and raised an eyebrow, and I could tell she knew how it felt to live with so much pressure from everyone.

"You're unsure of us? This courtship forced upon you?" she asked, and I could tell she was terrified.

"No, of course not," I said as I took her horse and tied her next to mine. "And... is it too much to say you impress me more after your riding ability was put on display?"

She took a step toward me and took my hand. My

heart raced when I felt the warmth of her fingers around me.

"Just wait until you see my riding ability on our wedding night," she said.

She drew me closer with bold initiative, and I couldn't get enough of her smell amidst all the hemlock and pine. I couldn't resist my urges anymore and leaned in, my mouth meeting hers.. She gave a surprised 'mmph' sound, and then I felt the soft strength in her arms as she wrapped them tighter around me.

I thought I'd hate myself for kissing another woman, but with her lips caressing mine, my heart screamed to my mind to proceed further with her. No royal manners, no propriety, just human instinct to never feel alone again.

Margaery's mouth opened, and the slightest prod of her tongue into my mouth put an end to my hesitation. I kissed her cheek, each peck getting softer and closer to her ear.

"Why wait for the wedding?"

With her strawberry blond hair in my face, I caressed the back of her head to feel the lustrous strands that cascaded down her back.

Red hair. Not quite as red as Lana's, though.

Her hips met mine, and I almost couldn't stand it. She had legs to get between, something Lana could not give me.

I'm sorry, I thought, pushing all thoughts of my Sea Fae maiden from my mind.

"The sun will be setting soon," I said. "Let me get a fire going."

Margaery surprised me when she helped gather wood. Smaller twigs, branches, and dried nettles for kindling. I found a dead hemlock and broke several branches.

With all the survival training I learned in my youth, I got the fire going as the stars came out through the pink and violet skies.

Not far away, I saw Margaery was lying on a patch of moss. She had her dress drawn up, just enough hanging between her legs to keep her womanhood hidden.

"I know you chose me," she said before showing me the patch of pale red between her legs. "But will you have me?"

I was glad we were alone. I knew all my advisors would insist on propriety, and I hated it.

Then I realized I was just standing there, not acting.

"My prince?" she asked.

I smiled. "No, my Lady. And... you can call me Alaric."

I knelt down between her feet.

"This isn't traditional, I'm sure," I said. "Quite honestly, I don't care. But perhaps you could honor one tradition only for me?"

"What is that?" Margaery asked.

I pulled off my shirt, feeling the cool mountain air clash with the fire's heat.

"A prince is supposed to ask. Will you have *me*, Margaery?"

I crawled on top of her, and she was illuminated by the orange fire and the silver moonlight.

"Anything for you, Alaric."

She put her hands on my face and drew me down for another kiss.

My hips could no longer resist, and I let my body-weight shift onto hers as her hands wrapped around my back.

So warm, I thought. *She is so warm.*

When she relented on my mouth, I moved down to kiss her neck, her collarbone, and swell of her breasts. Margaery surprised me with her strength when she rolled me onto the forest moss, which was cool on my back.

"Help me out of this cumbersome thing," she said. "Undo the laces on my back."

She shifted herself, so she was straddling me. I leaned up and with my arms around her as I fumbled with the straps until they loosened, helped her lift her dress over her head, revealing a thin chemise and nothing else but her femininity.

"You are the most beautiful thing I've ever seen," I said. But it was a lie. For all Margaery's beauty, she paled in comparison to the shimmering, ethereal grace of my Lana. But Lana was a dream and could never be anything more. Margaery was soft flesh and warm blood I could hold in my arms.

She pulled off the chemise, revealing her breasts, and I undid my trousers, exposing myself completely to her.

She neither looked impressed nor disappointed. All she did was kneel and crawl on top of me, warming me when skin met skin. Her hair spilled around our faces, giving me a veiled view of the sky above her, the campfire illuminating her light orange hair into curtains of shining embers.

When Margaery commenced kissing me again, I closed my eyes as I moved my hands up and down her spine, each time getting closer to the cleft of her buttocks. When I finally had handfuls of her backside, I pulled her hips to mine, and the warmth between her legs met my tip. The literal point of no return.

"Alaric," she sighed as she shifted her full weight on her hips, her flesh relenting to mine as I felt her envelop me entirely.

"Oh," I murmured.

"You may have me," she said as her hips lifted upward, just to take me inside her again. "Now, and forever."

She dug her fingernails into my shoulders, not enough to draw blood, but enough to hurt in a way I found alluring and playful.

My hands remained on her buttocks, and I used leverage from the forest floor to drive my hips harder and upward.

Each time I bucked, she met my rhythm. Then as her endurance began to wane, I pulled her down close and thrust harder.

She pivoted her back upward, and I moved my hands up to fondle her breasts. Her nipples were stiff in the cool air, and I kept them against my palms, which were still warm. I could feel her nervous heart pounding.

"It's alright," I said. "Don't be frightened."

She smiled and put her hands on either side of my shoulders.

Her moaning was soft at the beginning, but it grew into an indulgent whimper when I continued to drive inside her again and again.

Then I felt something incite within me. A growing pleasure crested, and I gasped when my body jolted, and her flesh felt warmer and wetter than before.

She gasped and looked down between our hips.

I haven't felt that good since laying eyes on Lana, I thought, and the moment would have been totally ruined were it not for Margaery's smile.

"My Alaric," she said as she moved to lie next to me.

For a few moments, we lay in silence, staring up at the clouds rolling rapidly across the sky. Then I stood and got my clothes. I lay my riding cloak next to the fire before putting my trousers back on.

Margaery added more wood and put her chemise back on.

We said nothing the rest of the night. She lay next to the fire, and I draped my arm over her as we slept under the moon.

I woke when the moon was at its apex, and the clearing was coated in silver light and walked away from the fire to relieve myself nearer to the creek rushing over the cliff.

The forest was illuminated, and I looked toward the sea. Lana's image flashed in my mind, and my heart tugged with uncertainty. Would I truly have to give up my dreams of her forever?

"It's a long way down if you take a bad step," Margaery's voice came from behind. She was wearing my cloak around her.

I said nothing and smiled.

"Was my... riding ability to your liking?"

"Oh, yes," I said. "But perhaps you'll be even better without racing horses beforehand."

She smiled. "Come back to the fire. Dawn's not for another four hours. We'll have to return to the castle before either of our parents panic at our being gone longer than a day without royal escorts."

Margaery kissed me again, and I was swept up by her perfumes, our sweat, and the smell of the forest.

We'll never be able to frolic with abandon like this again, I thought as I held her hand.

Again I couldn't help but think of the first time I met Lana. The night the ship sank, and waking up on shore with her beside me.

"You look worried about something," Margaery said.

"Choosing a wife is a big step," I said. "Only one of the hardest steps of my life. You wouldn't believe how easy it was to dismiss so many women, and now I find one who enthralls me like you. It's the biggest choice I've made so far, and..."

"I certainly hope you don't think you've chosen wrong after *everything* we did today," she said.

"No," I said. "It's just... marriage. It's so... final."

"Prince Alaric," she said. "If there is another woman, I demand to know now."

I winced. "No. There's nobody else."

She looked me up and down several times, waiting for any signs or tells that gave away my dishonesty. "If there was another you loved before, I promise I'll give you what she can't."

You're righter than you know, I thought.

"You are an exceptional woman, Margaery," I said. "And I know you will make an exceptional wife... mother... and queen one day."

All anger in her face washed away when joyous tears welled up.

I held her close, and I became rigid again as she commenced kissing my chest.

"I'll make you forget every girl besides me," she said as she kissed below my navel. "It's forgivable to have loved another. It will not be the same once we are married. There will be no need for whores, concubines, or any other women in your life except me."

I didn't protest. I didn't say anything as she took my rigid organ and kissed it before opening her mouth and wrapping her arms around my hips, digging her nails into the small of my back.

She lay on her back and beckoned me to lie on top of her.

This time I took all the knowledge I was advised with in terms of women's anatomy, and I remembered the pleasure treatises.

I rubbed between her legs, which I could tell she

enjoyed more than the act itself. Within a few minutes, she convulsed, and she covered her mouth to keep herself from screaming.

Margaery breathed deep, and her breasts heaved before she drew me downward. I forced my trousers down and entered her again, but I couldn't help but think of Lana. I looked into her eyes, but instead of Lana's golden hazel eyes, I saw Margaery's dark green eyes while my chosen bride-to-be was looking up at me.

I was betraying Lana, and my body relished every ravishing motion I gave to Margaery.

I gasped, and I finished again, my loins emitting wave after wave of my seed into her womb.

"I love you, Alaric," Margaery said before leaning up to kiss me. "You can do that whenever you wish, my prince."

We lay next to the fire, and she fell asleep before me. I tried to sleep, but I couldn't stop thinking about the two betrayals in one night.

Get over her, I thought. Love with Lana could not happen. Not like this. Not like with my future wife.

"Well, it seems I have no choice now," I began, a smile playing at my lips.

"Choice in what, Alaric?" she asked, brow furrowed in confusion.

"I've despoiled you." I hoisted myself to my knees and knelt before her. "So I must ask you to be my queen. Lady Margaery of Trystane, will you be my wife?"

Margaery's eyes welled with tears. For a moment, I feared I had overstepped, that this had all happened too soon, and she regretted our joining. Then she bobbed her head, and that radiant smile spread across her face.

"Oh, Alaric, of course! I thought you'd never ask."

I leaped to my feet, then bent, scooping Margaery in my arms and spinning around in a circle, holding her until she playfully swatted my arm and cried, "Alaric, you're making me dizzy."

With that, I set her down, planting another firm kiss on her lips. "Come," I said, "there's one more place I want to show you, then we'll head back to the castle. It's on the way."

I helped Margaery mount her horse, and we set off towards the shore. I brushed aside the tiny voice in my head that whispered, *Lana,* like a warning.

The trees grew sparse as we rode until their veil parted, revealing the brilliant blue of the sea and the silver shimmer of the white sands. The waters were calm, the dawn sky an overcast bruise-blue, but a few fissures in the clouds allowed sunbeams to slip through and pool in halos of light on the smooth glass-like surface. The rocky outcropping jutting up along the shoreline conjured images of Sea Fae, all wearing Lana's face, which I quickly cast aside.

"The sea is our livelihood here," I said, leading her down the steep protective dunes that lined the shore. "Nazure's oysters, cockles, and fish keep our people fed, and our pearl divers bring us great wealth. We are a small island kingdom, but our navy is unrivaled and our warships unsinkable." My lips fell into a frown as I remembered my sunken flagship, lost to the unnatural Fae waves. "Well, almost," I added as an afterthought.

"I always wondered how such a small kingdom could..."

Margaery continued, but her words were lost on me as we drew nearer to what I had assumed was a speck of driftwood washed ashore. Blood pounded in my ears, drowning out all other sounds, and my heart hammered against my ribcage. The lithe body, the shock of flame-red hair...

"Lana..." I whispered.

Margaery turned to me in confusion, but I kicked my horse, spurring it to a gallop towards the form of the girl – the Sea Fae – *Lana,* lying half-submerged on the beach. It was her. It had to be her. Who else had hair like that, a body like that? But what had happened to her?

When I reached her, I leaped off my horse and fell to the sand beside the woman's prone form. Her eyes were closed, her lips drawn into a grim line that made it clear she was okay. My heart sang and screamed in discordant harmony.

Reaching down, I laid a hand on the woman's naked breast, feeling the steady rise and fall, and let out a relieved breath. She was alive. Just then, her thick lashes fluttered, revealing the luminous pools of her icy blue eyes that I would have known anywhere.

"Lana, it is you," I whispered.

She blinked once and opened her mouth like she would speak, but no words came out. A single tear spilled down her cheek. I felt a warmth beside me and glanced up to see Margaery standing with her hands clasped, her face drawn in sympathy.

"Oh, poor dear, you must be half-frozen. Were you shipwrecked? Come, we will take you to the castle and get you help." She bent lower, extending a hand to the maiden lying on the sand.

"Margaery, she's a—" I dropped off, for, as Margaery helped the red-haired, blue-eyed woman who looked so very much like Lana to stand, I realized this could not be Lana. For where once her glorious tail had been, there were now long, slender legs.

"Alaric, do you know this girl?" Margaery asked as I moved into position to help support the injured girl's weight.

My mind reeled. She looked so very much like Lana, the Sea Fae who had rescued me. Yet, she could not be. She was just a girl. No mermaid's tail, no siren song. Just an uncanny resemblance.

"No," I said, the words coming out more sullen than I'd meant them to. "I mistook her for someone else." I frowned, uncertain because I was so sure... Then I shook my head. "Not the same girl. Come, let's get her back to the castle and have the healer look at her."

Lana

ALARIC... His name, I had that much at least. A tiny piece of his soul. *It is Lana who saved your life! I became this dreadful mortal* thing *for you,* I tried to tell him with my eyes. But he did not recognize me in the wretched new body the Old Gods had cursed me with. When he looked away, smiling tenderly at the woman who had arrived with him, my heart shattered in my chest.

I had felt so sure, so certain, that he had fallen for me in those brief moments we had spent on the shore that day. I was a Sea Fae... The ultimate enchantress. How could he not? But no. No longer. Now, I was just a girl. No different from the one who stood beside him. One who, I could tell, held a firm grip on his heart. *The one to whom his soul belongs,* a voice strangely like Ula's hissed in my ear.

My thoughts were silenced by the searing pain in my feet as Alaric and the woman led me up the long stretch of beach, my arms draped over their shoulders for support. A million daggers of pain lanced from heel to toe with each footfall. A silent sob wracked my body, and the unknown woman squeezed my shoulder gently.

"There now, whatever is wrong, we will have you fixed up. You'll be right as rain soon," she reassured me in a kind, sweet voice.

I wanted to scream at her that she was wrong. No mortal healer could fix what ailed me. That *she* was the grievance, not the unrelenting pain in my feet, and I did not want her sympathy. But I could not utter so much as a sound.

My agony was set aside for a moment as the castle came into view. Set atop a cliff overlooking a rocky stretch of shoreline, its white spires soared higher than even the gulls could fly. Red and gold pennons flew from the battlements, rippling in that same cool wind that assaulted my bare skin.

"Someone fetch the King's healer!" Alaric cried as two men clad in gleaming metal appeared at the gates, which opened with a sharp screech. Frightened, I flinched back, cowering.

"It's alright. They're my knights. They won't hurt you," Alaric assured me.

Still, I refused when he tried to usher me into their care. I had never seen armor. To me, these were not men but metal beasts. I shrieked soundlessly and clawed at Alaric, clinging to him desperately until he folded his arms around me. There, in his embrace, I felt safe again. I looked up in time to see his eyes meet the other woman's gaze apologetically before dropping back down to me.

"Margaery, see if you can find something for her to wear. She's very frightened, and see how she's shivering? I'll bring her inside to the fire. Roland,"—he turned to one of the men clad in metal—"We left our horses on the beach, send some men after them."

Alaric shifted positions, then lifted me into his arms, cradling me. The pain in my feet subsided at last.

"Of course," Margaery and Roland both said after a beat and an unreadable look exchanged between each other. Margaery's tone was bright, but it had a strained quality. I did not know, then, she was to be his wife. How she must have felt to see another beautiful woman held in his arms.

Margaery set off through the castle gates, Alaric behind her, carrying me. The man named Roland did not move. Situated as I was in Alaric's arms, I had a clear view of him scowling after us. The look on his face sent a shiver down my spine, so I dropped my head into the crook between Alaric's broad shoulder and his neck. He smelled of the sea and other things I did not yet know of. The smoke of the hearth, green leaves, and the mulch of the forest floor. But most of all, to me, at the moment, he smelled of the sea. Of home.

The fire sizzled and crackled, and I stared into it, never having seen such a thing before. The elderly man with the long gray beard and crinkled skin prodded and probed at me until at last, he let out a long, drawn-out sigh.

"There's nothing wrong with her, physically, that I can find," the healer said, frowning down at me. Margaery had returned with clothes, which he had dressed me in before the examination; a gown, which, while warm, scratched my delicate skin. I wanted to claw at my flesh and strip off the garment but was astute enough to sense that would not be acceptable etiquette here. Everyone around wore some manner of attire. The mortal world was nothing like the Sea Court, where we roamed freely wearing nothing but the skins the Goddess blessed us with.

Alaric rubbed his temples and sighed. "Obviously, there is something wrong. Can you not see that she's in pain? She can hardly walk. And what of her voice? Why can't she talk?"

The old grey-bearded healer sucked his teeth. "Perhaps a trauma of the mind?" He tapped his head. "Could be, in time, she will come around. But there's nothing more I can do for her than to give her a poppy draught to help her rest and recover."

"Fine, leave it there, then." Alaric scowled and gestured at a small table beside him.

The healer nodded, set the draught down, then bowed. "With your leave, my Prince. I'll be back to check on her in the morning."

Alaric nodded, and the man tottered from the room. When the healer had gone, Alaric turned his gaze on me again, studying me with smoldering eyes for a long moment, before sighing. "I wish you could tell me what ails you. And your name. Who you are and where you've come from."

I, too, longed to tell him all of these things. But I had no way to do so. Instead, I dropped my eyes back to the fire. There was a beat of silence between us before Alaric said, "You remind me of someone I once knew. Her name was Lana. Is it alright if I call you that for now?" he asked, brushing a strand of hair of damp hair behind my ear.

My heart leaped with joy, hearing him utter my name and I nodded my head, a smile spreading across my face.

His lips lifted in a returned smile. "You like that, do you? It's strange. You look so much like her." He stopped speaking, his eyes roving over me. Then he blinked and shook his head. "But no, it cannot be."

Oh, what I would have given to have my voice back, even just for one moment. To be able to tell him, "It *is* me, Alaric. I am Lana."

At the sound of a knock upon the door, Alaric called, "Come in," over his shoulder.

The door opened, and Margaery appeared. She smiled kindly at me then looked at Alaric with what I recognized as love in her eyes. And my insides twisted. This girl, dressed in a beautiful pale pink gown, her hair perfectly coiled, cheeks dusted with shimmering pink, was in love with my Prince too. It was as clear as day. And he, curse him, felt the same.

"I hope you're feeling better, dear heart," she said to me with such sincerity that it pained me. She seemed like a lovely girl. But I could not permit her to steal Alaric's heart. My life, my continued existence, my *immortality* were riding on Alaric. "You have some color back at least," she went on, then she turned to Alaric. "Dinner is ready in the hall, my love. Will you be joining us?"

Alaric hesitated, his eyes flitting from Margaery to me then back again to where she stood in the doorway. "We'll both join you." As Alaric reached down to take my hand, I saw a shadow pass across Margaery's face again. Jealousy. And guilt for that jealousy.

With Alaric's help, I got to my feet. I immediately gasped. The pain had not diminished. Noticing my discomfort, the prince reached for the vial the healer had left behind. "Here, drink this down. It should help."

After the last potion I had drunk, I was wary of the draught, but the pain was such that I would do anything to ease it. So I took the bottle and drank it in one quick swallow.

"You'll feel better soon." Alaric gave me a bright smile, and we walked together, side by side, him supporting me with an arm wrapped around my shoulder. Margaery walked ahead of us and was the first through the vaulted doorway that led to the great hall.

Stepping through, dozens of eyes all went to us and held there, sending a shiver of fear coursing through me. Though I had often entertained in my father's halls, this felt entirely different. So many mortals, all strangers to me, and a confused din rose, reverberating through the room. Though the words were hushed, I immediately understood the cause. They were surprised to see me by

Alaric's side, not Margaery. I forced the smirk that threatened to emerge away from my face and dropped my eyes to the floor.

My pulse pounded in my temples, and I was afraid I might faint when suddenly a warmth washed over me, like the southern currents that flowed through the currents of the Sea Court. The pain in my feet eased, and the world took on a haziness. I felt blissfully detached from it all and let out a sigh of relief.

Approaching the head of the large rectangular table positioned in the center of the room, Alaric said, "Roland, move down a seat for Lady Lana." His voice was calm, but his tone imparted it as a command, not a request. The man to Alaric's left, who I had not recognized as the same man clad in iron at the castle gates, gave me a long look and raised his brows but obliged, moving down a seat.

I all but collapsed into the now vacant seat where he had been as the man called Roland said, "Well met, my Lady. And who might you be?"

Something was cutting in his tone, and his dark eyes had narrowed to accusatory slits, lines pinching the skin around him to make him appear older than he was. His cold look pervaded through the haze of the draught I had drunk to send a shiver through me.

"She cannot speak," Alaric explained on my behalf.

"And why is that?"

"Shock, the doctor thinks. But she will soon recover, I'm sure of it." Alaric gave me a pat on the hand and a kind smile, but his brother only snorted disdainfully.

"Shock. Yes, I'm sure that's it." Sarcasm laced his words.

I knew at that moment that though this man did not know me, he hated me.

Silence pervaded. Alaric on one side of me cast a daggered glare at Roland on the other, and I feared that they might come to blows. Blessedly, the food arrived at that moment, diffusing the mounting tension. But I grimaced at the platters arrayed on the table. Oysters, clams, and cockles, several varieties of whole fish, their dead eyes staring accusingly at me. In the Sea Court, we lived on seaweed, kelp, seagrass. These creatures were our friends.

Roland was the first to notice my discomfort. "Do you not eat the bounty of the sea, Lady Lana?" he asked with a sneer. "What a surprise."

He knows, I realized. *He knows what I am.* I ought to have been happy. If he knew, he might tell Alaric, who would then realize himself what I was. But the cruel twist of his lips sent a stab of terror through me.

I reached for a plate with a shaking hand and put a small portion of fish upon it. I watched the others as they lifted the small devices with metal prongs, much like miniature versions of my father's trident, and began using it to spear their fish. I took a bite. It stuck in my throat, but thanks to the draught the healer had given me I felt an unusually calm indifference and was able to force it down.

Margaery and Alaric chatted beside me through the meal, while Roland cast me occasional indifferent glances. I tried to let it roll off until, finally, the plates were cleared. I hoped that would be the end of it, and I could retire somewhere to rest, but it wasn't to be so.

After the meal, the minstrels in the back of the hall began to play. The music was strange and foreign to me. We had no harps or fiddles in the Court of Sea, only our sweet voices and those of the whales and dolphins to join in our serenades. I watched, astonished, as the men and women around me rose to their feet and took to the floor in the center of the room, Margaery and Alaric included.

Together they twirled and spun, their feet tapping out elaborate rhythms on the hard stone floor. My eyes stayed glued to Alaric, the way his gaze followed Margaery's every move. As if she was an enchantress. *If I could do that, I could win his heart,* I thought,

"Lady Lana, do you not dance?" Roland, who hadn't taken the floor with the others, suddenly probed.

I shook my head, casting my eyes down. *Not yet. But I will.*

Alaric

AFTER THE MEAL, Margaery and I escorted Lady Lana to her chambers. Weary from whatever she had undergone and the healer's draught, she fell asleep the moment her head hit her pillows. I drew the blankets up around her chin and studied her. The almost unnaturally pale ivory of her skin, the striking scarlet hair. So strange. *Are you a Fae? Are you my Lana from the beach?* I silently demanded. But of course, she did not answer.

"Alaric, let's leave her to rest," Margaery suggested, drawing my attention as she took me by the hand.

I rose from where I knelt and nodded, following Margaery out of the room. I suddenly felt stricken by guilt. The woman beside me had given herself to me today, body and soul. Pledged herself in marriage and allowed me to take her maidenheadd on the forest floor. And yet, all I could think about was this other girl.

I suddenly stopped and drew her close to me, gazing down at her rosy-cheeked face in the flickering torchlight of the corridor. "I'm sorry our adventure ended the way it did, Margaery."

She gave me a gentle smile. "There is nothing to apologize for. If anything, you have shown me that, in your heart, you are a good and kind man. It isn't every lord who would take a nameless castaway into their home and feed them at their hearth as you've done."

I sighed, Margaery's unwavering faith in me making me feel guiltier still. But before I could respond, a gruff clearing of the throat sounded behind me.

"Alaric, we must speak." I stiffened, recognizing that it was Roland at once from the somber inflection in his voice. He was the last person I wanted to speak with, especially after his behavior towards Lana at dinner. But I also knew he would give me no peace until we had words.

"Margaery, it has been a lovely evening. I'll break the news of our engagement to my father this evening." I shot Alaric a pointed look, already aware of the topic he meant to discuss.

Margaery curtsied and smiled graciously. "I shall see you in the morrow, my love," she said, then swept down the hall towards her chambers.

As soon as she was out of sight, I turned to my brother. "What?" I snapped.

Roland didn't beat around the bush. "Who is this girl you pulled from the sea? Why bring her here? She clearly isn't high born." He turned his nose up and sniffed as if he smelled something foul.

I took him by the shoulder and stared him down. "Roland, the girl was injured—"

He cut me off with, "That's not what the healer says."

"The healer is a fool," I growled.

"She's a Fae!" Roland shot back.

I blinked at him, shocked. "What? She is just a girl!"

Roland snorted. "Stay away from her, Alaric. Or I'll feed her back to the sea where she belongs myself."

With that, he turned and walked away, leaving me to brood on his words, which left me in a tailspin. Was Lana truly *my* Lana? A Sea Fae somehow in disguise?

It doesn't matter, I told myself. *I am promised to Margaery. I will not betray her.* And for many long days, I did not.

In the days that followed, we brought my father and his advisors the news of our engagement. They were pleased, as it was a strong diplomatic union, although my father seemed a bit perplexed.

"But I'm to marry Ylain," he kept insisting.

I did not know who Ylain was. He was not speaking of my mother, Estrella; that was for certain. My curiosity was piqued, but before I could ask further questions, the Master at Arms interrupted Father's prattle, booming, "Not your wedding, you damned old fool! Your son's!"

My father bowed his head. His lips trembled as he muttered, "Make sure you love her, son. A wedding without love is an abomination to the Goddess. She will curse you for it as they have me."

With that, I was swept from his chambers as if I were still a schoolboy. But I did not protest. It pained me to see my father in his fallen state.

And so ensued a period of feasting and travel, visiting all the far corners of the realm to alert my people of the marriage that would take place in three weeks' time. When our union was announced to the smallfolk, they were jubilant. They loved the beautiful Lady Margaery from the rich land across the sea. In every town and seaside village, they chanted our names and offered toasts in our name.

Such was the hoopla that I was able to put Lana almost completely from my mind. Almost. I still felt the tug of guilt at leaving her abandoned, far from home, wherever that was, essentially locked away in her quarters in my castle. But she was well cared for by the healer, I was sure, and had any comfort she should require at her disposal.

It wasn't until Margaery came to my chambers on the last night of our ventures through the countryside that I allowed my lust for her to creep back into my mind.

"Alaric," Margaery said, planting a light kiss on my brow.

I rose and wrapped my soon-to-be-wife in a warm embrace. "Margaery, what brings you to my chambers at this late hour?"

She chuckled. "My Lord, it's barely evening."

I glanced at the window. She was right. I was so weary from all the festivities and travel that it felt closer to midnight. "It seems I am growing too old for all of this fanfare," I said with a wan smile.

"It is nearly over now, only the wedding left to survive." She ruffled my hair playfully. I could feel my cock stir within my trousers but knew I dare not act upon it. Not until we were wed. Not within the walls of the castle, where eyes were everywhere. "I'll be returning to Trystane tomorrow."

My face must have fallen with this news, for Margaery immediately burst out laughing. "My love, only for a couple of days. I must gather my belongings and prepare for our life together." She brushed her lips against mine in a chaste kiss, the kind our advisors would not be scandalized by. I wanted more, so much more, but I dare not risk tarnishing her good name with unsavory rumors, so instead, I brushed a lock of hair behind her ear and kissed her on her forehead.

"I'm not sure how I'll survive here without you," I played it up for her, and she swatted me playfully on the shoulder.

"You made it through twenty-seven years before we met. I suspect you can make it through a few days more."

I shook my head in mock desperation, a smile toying at my lips. "It will be very, very difficult."

I knew it was horrible, but my thoughts went to Lana as soon as she left the room. But I did not go to see her until Margaery had left for Trystane. I told myself it was merely to check up on her, to ensure that she had everything she needed.

But I knew the truth. I wanted Lana, engaged or not.

Lana

Day after day, I spent alone in my chambers. Occasionally, the doctor would come to examine me. I dreaded his appearance. His frustration at my continued pain and lack of words grew more and more palpable with each visit. I was relieved when it reached a point where he stopped checking on me altogether and simply left the poppy draught on my bedside table.

Alaric did not visit. It seemed he had forgotten me completely. So I drank the poppy draughts, and I languished, tracking the Moon Goddess as she drifted lazily across the sky each night, counting down the days until my imminent demise. Trying desperately to think of a way to win Alaric's heart, should I ever have a chance to see him again.

Recalling that first night in the great hall, I realized I had never seen Alaric look on Margaery with such love as when she had danced for him. It would pain me greatly, but I had the draughts. I would learn to dance as she did, and I would win his heart away from her. And then I would claim his soul.

I took the crystalline bottle in my hands and swallowed it down, then waited a few moments for it to take effect, staring into the fire. When I felt the hazy warmth begin to drift over me, I rose from the settee.

At first, I attempted to mimic the steps I had seen Margaery and the other women perform in the dance hall. But they were so foreign to me, and I couldn't remember them all. So, instead, I began to create my own dance. Ignoring the ache coursing through my legs, I began to move my body to the music of the sea that was forever in my heart. I became the swift-moving currents, the languid waves at low tide, the powerful breakers ushered in my thunderheads.

A knock sounded upon the door, but I could not stop. I was lost in the dance of my gone world. I did not even turn towards it when I heard it creak open. It wasn't until I heard Alaric murmur, "Oh, Lana," that I paused and turned to face him.

He stood in the doorway, his sandy hair hanging loose to his shoulders. Margaery was not beside him. The candles danced, throwing shadows that ringed his emerald eyes and the salt and pepper scruff on his chin. He took a step forward, crossed the threshold, and then reached behind him to close the door.

"Dance for me, Lana," Alaric whispered.

I fought back a grimace. My legs were already close to seizing with pain. But I needed him to fall in love with me, and if this was the way to his heart, then so be it. I had told Ula that I would do whatever it took, and I meant to do just that.

In my mind, I conjured the melody of the sirens. And I danced again. Through the pain in my legs that I thought would break me, biting my lip to hold back the tears that threatened to spill, I pirouetted and spun, swaying my hips to the imagined beat of the tides breaking on the shore.

Alaric's eyes never left me, following each movement, utterly rapt, until I collapsed to the floor, my useless legs finally giving out completely. Moments later, I felt the warmth of his body beside me, then his strong arms as he lifted me from the floor and carried me to my bed, setting me upon it.

He leaned over me, his breath warm on my skin, close to my face. I reached for him, trailing my fingers along the hard line of his jaw, feeling the dusting of fine stubble there. My touch drifted down the curve of his neck to his chest, where a spattering of sandy hair poked out from his tunic. He shifted closer, our mouths just inches apart, sharing the same air.

"I shouldn't have come here," he murmured, but he didn't back away. Instead, he moved his hands to my temples, running his fingers through the long tangles of my hair. He twirled the edges around his palms, stroking the curls with his thumbs, and staring. Just staring at me with haunted eyes.

Then he went on, "I wish you could tell me who you are and how you came to be here. You're so very beautiful. I think... I think I would throw it all away. The marriage. The alliance. Everything. If I knew you were who I think you are." Our gazes were locked. We were trapped, unable to break away. My lips parted to whisper his name, but no sound came out.

I could kiss him now, I realized. *I could kiss him right now, and his soul would be mine.* But would it? Was I his true love, or was Margaery?

I decided I needed more time to ensure that his heart truly belonged to me. What would happen if our lips were to touch and I was *not* his one true love? Still, I would not waste this opportunity. Instead of kissing his mouth, I shifted slightly and ran my tongue slowly along the sensitive skin behind his ear, nibbling gently.

A low moan escaped his lips. "We shouldn't do this," Alaric whispered, his breath warm against my throat. Nevertheless, his tongue darted out, tracing a slow, meandering line down to the space between my breasts as his fingers traced my cheekbone.

His movement was sudden when he pulled me close to him. I felt the rise and fall of his chest pressed to the swell of my breasts and the firmness of his manhood against my inner thigh. "I want you." His hands came around, taking me the wrists and pinning me to the bed.

I blinked up at him, my whole body trembling with desire. But when he moved to kiss my mouth, again I turned away, so his lips fell upon the curve of my neck. He freed one of my hands as he fumbled with the lacings of his breeches, then took my face a little roughly and turned my head to face him.

"Do you want this as much as I do?" he asked, his voice husky with desire.

Slowly, I nodded my head. His cock dipped into my pussy, and his hand released my face, falling to my pearl and rubbing with quick, deft movements.

"And are you my Lana? The Sea Fae maiden who saved me?"

Yes, I mouthed soundlessly, nodding furiously. My body seized as he entered me fully, pounding as relentlessly as the storm-blown waves hammered the shore. Heat coiled up in my belly, threatening to explode, to tear me inside out, and I opened my mouth in a silent but primal scream when he spilled his seed on my belly.

Spent, he withdrew himself from me and laid beside me on the bed, his strong arms,

He left sometime in the night, and I awoke to find myself alone, the fire burning low, the first rays of dawn streaming through my window. My body was sore, and my thoughts were filled with doubt.

If I had only kissed him, I thought, *once he knew who I was.*

But to do so would have killed him, and as much as I still yearned for an immortal soul beyond all else, I couldn't bring myself to do it.

There will be other chances, I told myself.

And I was right.

Alaric

I STOOD on the castle battlements, watching the surf churn, angry and relentless. I had not seen Lana since that night. I told myself I just needed some time to sort through my feelings. I had told her I would throw it all away for her. But could I? To reject the alliance with Trystane after swearing my hand to Margaery would be an affront that Margaery's father, and her people, would not soon forget. Not to mention my own people. Oh, how they loved sweet, pretty Lady Margaery. How would they take to someone like Lana? As distant, silent, and strange as the Moon Goddess herself.

Yet as soon as I had renewed my commitment to Margaery in my mind, my father's words sounded. *A wedding without love is an abomination to the Goddess. She will curse you for it.* Did I love Margaery? Perhaps, in a way. She was pleasing to look at, spirited, and confident. She would certainly make the perfect queen. But there was not the same magic as with Lana, whom I was drawn to like a planet in orbit around a sun.

Frustration was setting in, and I slammed my hand against the stone wall, only to hear a quiet tsk from behind me. Roland.

"I should have thought you'd be rejoicing. Your fiancé's ship is due today, is it not?" He stood with hands clasped in front of him. It seemed that even in the brief days since we'd last spoken, his face had grown more pinched, his hairline receding farther back from his face

"I am not sure I am ready to marry," I answered stiffly, turning away from him to stare at the deep indigo of the ocean reflecting only clouds above. A sharp breeze kicked up, and I could feel the first touch of winter riding aloft on it.

Roland snorted. "What is there to be sure of? You've already taken her if the whispers I've heard are to be believed. You should know—"

I whirled on him and cut him off, grabbing the collar of his doublet. "Where did you hear that?"

Roland wrenched himself free of my grasp and scowled. "Surely you don't think the advisors let the two of you gallivant unescorted all over the kingdom without a watchful eye." My heart plunged into my belly, and my guts churned, but my brother wasn't done yet. "What if you planted a seed in her belly, Alaric? Will you return her to Trystane as a ruined woman? And for what? A Fae whore?"

My first impulse was to deck him in the face for speaking such words about Lana. But I knew that would not accomplish anything, so I balled my hands into fists at my sides, so tight that my nails cut into the flesh of my palms. "She isn't a whore."

"But she *is* a Fae, isn't she?"

I remained silent.

"You have to marry Margaery, brother. Fae or otherwise, no will accept that strange, silent, foreign woman as the queen. Not the advisors, not Father, and not the people of your kingdom. So you can stand out here in the cold and brood as long as you'd like. But I would hope, in the end, you put your country about that siren slut."

Roland didn't give me time to respond before turning on his heel and storming back into the castle. He was right, I knew. To renege on the promise to wed Margaery would not only break her heart but could destroy our entire kingdom if Trystane sought revenge for the wrong.

I sighed, turning my gaze from the water. I would have to break the news to Lana, but I didn't know how to do it. My heart burned as if it was on fire, and there was nothing to quench the ache, not even the vast sea. Only the beauty who had come from it, but I could not go to her. I knew what would happen.

So, I decided to continue avoiding her at least until after the wedding.

* * *

"Alaric, my love, what's wrong? Are you ill?" Margaery traced the dark shadows that hung under my eyes with a finger, her face a mask of concern.

I shook my head and forced a smile. "No, my dear. The wedding preparations have just been grueling."

She laughed, a heartfelt sound that should have warmed my frozen heart but did nothing to ease the cold dread that pounded with each beat of it. "I thought I was unlucky to have to leave your side and return to Trystane, but perhaps it was luck indeed. I'm sorry you had to bear the burden of the arrangements, my dear."

"It is a small thing when I know that when this is all through, we will be joined to one another for a lifetime." Somehow I forced the words out without choking on them, though they stuck in my throat.

Margaery smiled, and for a moment, I felt that love for her I felt that night on the cliffs, before Lana had come into our lives, rush back to me. She sat down at the table and pulled her long strawberry hair free of its knot, sending it cascading over her shoulders in a river. "And how is our friend, that dear girl whom you plucked from the sea?"

There was no malice in her tone. Margaery wasn't the sort to mince words or thinly veil her intentions. I knew that. She was genuinely curious but talking about Lana with her only set me more on edge.

"She still cannot speak. But her legs seem to be doing better." My mind drifted to the vision of her dancing alone in her room, a dance unlike any I had ever seen.

One so alluring that I had lost my senses and given in to my lust. Guilt stabbed me in the guts like a saber.

"You've invited her to the wedding, haven't you?" Margaery asked, running a comb through her hair to smooth the tangles of the wind-swept boat trip from it.

I quickly had to rearrange my features to remove the mask of horror they'd fallen into. "I – uh – it hadn't occurred to me."

Margaery turned from the mirror and frowned at me. "The poor thing needs a bit of joy in her life. Go invite her, love. I'm sure she will enjoy being there for the festivities instead of cooped up in that drafty room."

I swallowed hard. I did not want to go to Lana. I feared what I would do when faced with her. But I also needed to get away from Margaery and the guilt that was threatening to swallow me whole, so I nodded and said, "A wonderful idea, my love. I was so preoccupied with making the arrangements it must have slipped my mind. How thoughtless of me."

Then I strode from the room.

* * *

I should have knocked. Perhaps she would have been more prepared. Instead, I flung the door open and walked in to find her dancing again. Her body moved with an unnatural fluidity, bending in ways no mortal girl's body ever could. I was mesmerized, caught in a spell that went unbroken until, at the sound of the door opening, she froze mid-pirouette and turned to me with a hungry desperation in her eyes that caused my breath to hitch in my throat.

She rushed towards me. Without looking behind, I slammed the door closed and moved to meet her in the middle of the room, catching her in my arms. She had grown thinner. Her bones felt hollow as a bird's jutting through her skin, which had grown so pale it was almost translucent. Such a change in just a week since I had last seen her. Since we had...

I wiped the memory of our coital bliss from my mind. "Lana," I said, leading her over to the settee near the fire. I noticed the rows of empty crystalline vials lined up along the table beside her bed and wondered if the poppy was what accounted for the change in her. "We need to talk."

I sat down beside her and placed my hands on either side of her face, cupping her gaunt face. "Tomorrow, I am to marry Margaery," I said, my voice coming out shakier than I had intended.

When the tears fell from her eyes, any illusions I had as to her origins were shattered. It was not water that leaked from those stormy blue orbs but tiny pearls that fell to the ground like bits of crystal shattering on the stones.

She shook her head wildly, then brought her hands to her head and ripped them through her scarlet curls, silent sobs overtaking her body. I grabbed both of her wrists in a move that instantly brought our night together back to me. So intense was the memory and the lust it brought with that that once I held her there, I froze. How would I ever pull away?

It took everything in me to master myself, release her, and say, "Lana. You and I cannot be. I'm promised to another. But you will always have a place here. I will keep you safe forever. I will love you forever."

She moved to kiss me then. She smelled of the deep sea and forgotten coves, and her eyes were like two pools trying to pull me in, to drown me and steal me away from this world forever.

But I pulled away. And when I did, she gave me a slow shake of her head, then rose and, hobbling as if in great pain, made her way to the bed and turned to face the wall.

Lana

THE FAE DO NOT WED, we are Bound to our mates, but still, I knew what Alaric was saying. Though he loved me, he would never belong to me. I was not his true love, and when he pulled away, I knew... there would be no kiss.

Alaric did not come to my bedside. I heard his footsteps drawing away and the soft click of the door as it closed behind him.

Two days. That was all the time I had left before the Old Gods came and reaped their reward for my failure. My greatest fear, the nothingness, the Void, was bearing down on me, and it seemed there would be no escape.

I laid there all through the night until the Moon Goddess had hidden away once more. When a knock sounded on the door, and a woman who introduced herself as one of Margaery's ladies walked in, I only nodded my consent as she began to dress me. It wasn't the itchy wool shift I was accustomed to. This was a lovely gown like the ones Margaery wore. It was a deep shade of violet, form-fitted to the ankles, then flaring, and it reminded me of my beautiful shimmering tail. Another thing I had forsaken in my futile quest for immortality.

"You look right pretty, though a bit sickly. I hear you're from abroad. Don'tcha like the food here?" Margaery's woman chirped.

I didn't answer, just stared into the mirror at my waifish body and sallow skin. I looked as if I was already disappearing. Turning to seafoam before my own eyes.

The woman let out a long, drawn-out sigh, then took me by the elbow. She led me through the halls of the palace. Presumably busy with the same festivities as everyone else, the healer had left me no draught of poppy. My bones felt as if they were made of glass that might shatter with each step; a thousand tiny needles pierced the balls of my feet.

When we made it to the castle gate, there was no sign of Alaric or Margaery. Only one of Alaric's metal men, standing beside a horse. He gave me a cursory look up and down, then spoke. "You aren't looking well, Lady Lana."

I recognized the voice at once. Roland, Prince Alaric's brother. The man who so despised me. I was struck with terror for a brief moment. I did not want to ride beside this man. But then... I would be gone soon, could already feel myself fading away. So what did I have to fear from him?

I let him help me on the horse, sitting astride it in

front of him. I was sure he would throw me from the beast to be rid of me. Instead, he leaned close and whispered in my ear, "I know what you are, and I know what you wanted to do. Seduce my brother. I only wish I could ask you why. Well, I suppose I could. But you can't answer, can you?"

If I could have spoken, I would have told him, *I had a chance to steal Alaric's soul, and I did not do it. You may hate me for what I am, but you should thank me for that. He lives because I withheld my kiss. I truly do love him, although he loves another.*

But I could not speak. So I remained silent as we cantered down the beach to the ship where Alaric's wedding was to take place. It was wrought of golden-hued wood. At its prow, a figurehead that caused my breath to catch in my throat. Carved from pale white birch, the flowing-haired maiden was plainly a replication of myself. A new ship, freshly made to replace the flagship my Aunt Ula had sunken. *Oh, Aunt Ula. You tried to warn me. You were right the whole time. Why was I so headstrong?*

Even Ula could not help me now. I had no way to reach her, and she had warned me of the cost of failure.

Roland led me up the narrow gangplank and onto the ship, my steps stilted by my aching legs. The buzz of celebration was in the air, along with the scent of fried fish that turned my belly to rubber. A flower-strewn arch had been erected on the ship's main deck, and beneath it stood Margaery and Alaric. Margaery's pale hair was piled up in a loose chignon, stray waves framing her rosy, heart-shaped face. She looked so very *happy* standing there, beaming her white-toothed smile at my lover. Alaric, looking splendid as ever in a fine satin tunic, smiled as well, although there was a forced quality to it.

He does not want to marry her, I realized suddenly.

As if reading my mind, Roland wrenched my shoulder roughly, spinning me around. "Don't you dare do a thing to interfere. The country needs her. Alaric needs her. We do not need the likes of you." With that, he shoved me and walked away. I crashed into the wooden railing and found myself gazing into the calm waters. Staring at a home that I could never return to. I began to cry, the pearls of my tears falling into the shallows, the plinks of them hitting the water drowned out by a cacophony of applause on the deck.

And then I heard something that caught me by surprise. "Lana," a chorus of voices called from the deep. A symphony of siren songs beckoning me. My sisters' voices. Their faces appeared beneath the surface, all gazing up at me.

"Lana, there is another way," Marina, the youngest of my siblings, whispered. She reached up towards me, something glittering in her hand.

"Stab his false lover in the heart. Spill her blood and feed it to the waves. Then, you will be free to return to us and live out your days in the Court of Sea," Tasi went on.

"Ula says it is so," Azurine added, and all the others echoed her words, "It is so..."

I reached down, grabbing the pearl-studded pommel of the silver blade. It was tiny, no longer than my ring finger, and, darting my eyes around to ensure no one was watching, I slipped the sheathed dagger into my bodice. My heart beat fast against the cold metal pressed to my breast.

"Lana!" a voice called out to me. I spun around to see Margaery. She was trotting towards me in her elaborate confection of a gown, a wide smile stretched across her face, arms held out as if she would draw me close in an embrace. "I'm so glad you were able to make it. Isn't it wonderful to be out of those stuffy halls in the fresh air?"

She was presenting me with a golden opportunity.

I raised my hand, prepared to lash out at Margaery with the dagger, to do as my sisters and Ula had bidden me and feed her warm, sweet blood to the ocean and return at last to my home. From the corner of my eye, I saw movement – Roland rushing towards me, calling Margaery's name. He had seen the blade, but I still had time.

I lunged. Margaery's scream laced the air, mingling with Roland's and now Alaric's too. But the knife did not find home. Instead, I twisted my wrist, hurling it overboard. I could not do it. To kill her would be to spill the blood of an innocent. Margaery was guilty of no crime, save loving the same man as me. She was his promised. I had no claim on him.

I took a last fleeting look around. Alaric had frozen upon seeing the dagger go overboard, and he stood with wide, bewildered eyes, staring at me beside his bride. I gave him a last wistful smile and then called out, "Alaric. I loved you." This time the words came.

Unlike his brother, Roland had not slowed his pace as he barreled towards me. Moments before he reached me, I threw a kiss on the wind to Alaric, and then I followed after the blade, leaping over the railing and into the cold, familiar embrace of the sea.

My home. I had returned, even if only for a moment.

Epilogue

I HAD HEEDED the call of the Void and expected to be met with my greatest fear: nothingness. But it was not nothingness that greeted me when I opened my eyes. Nor was it my father's watery halls. It was the warm kiss of the sun against my skin. I found myself suspended as if hovering above the world, floating on lazy currents that moved me closer and closer to the golden orb of the sun.

"The Old Gods of the Blood would claim you for the Void." The voice that spoke had a playful lilt to it, and I blinked into the brightness, trying to make out the speaker, but I saw only the blinding radiance of the sun.

"It is only fair. I was warned of the cost of failure."

Laughter sounded around me, coming from all directions at once. "And yet... you stayed your hand. You could have killed the girl and returned to your home. You did not. Why?"

I lifted my shoulders in a shrug. "It would have been

wrong. Just as it would have been wrong to steal Alaric's breath with a kiss, even if I could have. I – I just couldn't do it," I stammered as the warmth intensified, enveloping me. "Who are you? Where am I?"

Laughter again. "The Old Gods are not the only ones who look over you, Lana, of the Court of Sea. I saw the sacrifice you made and have brought you to my domain to offer you a gift. A new Geis, of a sort."

I was immediately wary. If I had learned one thing, it was that one should never take a Geis lightly. "What sort of gift?" I asked, uncertain.

"I would take you as a Demi-Goddess of sorts. A spirit. You will ride the winds, however far they will take you and bask in my rays until the end of your Fae days. You will feel the warmth of my touch wherever you may wander. All I ask in return is for the remainder of your life to be spent in servitude."

I frowned. "To you?"

"No. To mankind. Three hundred years, I ask of you. Aid the desolate and fallen, the lost and mournful amongst the mortals. Be their succor and comfort. That is all you will need to do."

"And when three hundred years have passed?" I pressed, not wanting to make the same mistake I had made once before.

"You will get that which you desire most in this world."

Immortality. The word rang out in my mind, but I simply said, "A soul?"

There was a flash of blue light, and I could make out the form of the Goddess for just a moment as she said, "Yes, Lana. I will grant you an immortal soul."

One Wish

One

KOSHAGAL. Glimmering jewel of the desert. A patchwork of red roofs suspended over an ancient harbor whose mosques rose incandescent against the Kaspian sea. The sunsets, pomegranate bright, dripped over drydocks, and merchant ships moored along the quay. Catamarans skimmed across an azure slice of the ocean while fishmongers lingered on the wharves. A city where vast stretches of barren sand coalesced into the majesty of a seaside metropolis. Koshagal's domes, arches, and spires soared like a multicolored mirage behind sandstone walls etched with words of power.

This had once all belonged to Yasmina, the only child of the Sultan, heir to the throne. Then Jaffar had fooled them all, emerging from the lamp in which he had been trapped. A free Djinn, more powerful than ever.

Now, Yasmina crept soundlessly through alleys, feet bare and calloused, footsteps light. She'd traded her silks and jewels for the ragged garb of an urchin. No one looked twice at a drifter in Koshagal. Not under Jaffar's rule, a tyranny that left the people starving. The poor were everywhere, beggared by his greed, barely surviving on the scraps leftover after paying tribute every month. Gold was scarce. Food, even scarcer. Joy, scarcer still.

But Yasmina's belly hungered for more than the sustenance food could bring her. She craved revenge, and her desire for it ate away at her guts more than the starvation did. So, invisible, she stalked the shadows, half-feral, seeking the one who could help her reclaim what she had lost. At least some of it. Other things... well, they would never be restored. Like her heart.

She was close now, though. So close. *Find the Seer, the mystic. Where the groves of olive trees shadow the streets and the sun crests the city walls at daybreak. Look to the doors for the mark of the witch. She will help you. I love you. I'm sorry. I'm yours always.* Alladin's parting words, spoken on his last breath, came back to her. Yasmina knew they were in the right part of the city now. She need only find the right door.

A scuffling noise sounded behind Yasmina, and she whirled to face it, relieved to see only a small creature scuttling across the sun-baked ground. It leaped, chittering, onto Yasmina's shoulder, long tail wrapping around her neck for purchase.

"Banu," she scolded the little monkey. "You'll strangle me."

The creature babbled incoherently, which Yasmina took for an apology, then unwrapped its tail from around her throat and swung around, perching on her outstretched hands.

"Did you find the Seer's door?" she asked.

Banu cocked his head, nodding once.

"Are you sure?"

Banu gave her a look like she was the world's biggest fool and nodded to her again.

"Alright. I hope you're right this time. Will you show me the way?" She rumpled the fur on his forehead good naturedly.

Banu twittered irritably at Yasmina and groomed his fur so that it lay flat on his head once more. Then he bounded out of her arms. With a jerk of his head, the monkey indicated an alleyway between two buildings and scampered ahead of Yasmina. The passage smelled of piss and refuse, but so did she, by this point. She had wandered the city for weeks, seeking the Seer, and Banu had been wrong before. She only hoped this time he had truly found the right door as she followed the little monkey until he stepped out of the shadowed darkness and onto a narrow lane.

Yasmina emerged to stand beside Banu and glanced furtively around. She was ever alert for those that tracked her, for the knives in the dark that sought to end her claim to the throne. Even disguised as a peasant, as she was, the wrong pair of eyes might recognize her. Jaffar had to know neither he nor his reign was safe, so long as breath remained in her lungs and her heart pumped blood through her veins. He had to know she would seek retribution. And Jaffar's eyes were everywhere.

But there was no sign of assassins or guards here. A few half-starved children tossed knucklebones in the street, and a pensive woman with a drawn, weary face hung laundry on a line in a courtyard. The red and yellow fabric wafted in the dry, hot breeze like brightly colored flags. A stark contrast to the crumbling facades of the timeworn sandstone buildings. The city walls rose in the distance, tall and imposing, marked with magic to stave off invaders. Alas, they had done little to protect the city from enemies within.

Banu tugged at Yasmina's leg, then gesticulated towards a door across the lane with a five-pointed star emblazoned upon it. The witch's mark. Just as Aladin had described it. Her hands became sweaty as her heart thudded a beat like the drums of war pounding inside her chest. Was this the place? Would she at last find what she sought?

For a moment, Yasmina hesitated, fearing what lay beyond that door. She had never met a Magi before. The wise women were both revered and feared by her people for their power. Taking a deep breath, she steeled herself and tugged her ragged cidaris lower on her face to obscure it. Keeping her eyes downcast, she crossed the street. Upon approaching the door, she raised the brass knocker. It sounded with a resonant boom that made her shudder. Yasmina waited, but there was only silence. She lifted the knocker again and let it fall. At first, there was still no response. Then Yasmina heard shuffling footsteps from within.

"Who seeks Anahita's wisdom?" a frail, quivering voice inquired.

Yasmina fidgeted. Her name was like a precious gemstone that she guarded with her very life. She did not want to utter it aloud on the streets of this city to this stranger behind a closed door.

"I am a friend of Aladin," she finally replied.

With that, locks clicked within, and the door creaked open. An old woman peered out, bent and bowed, with skin the texture of old parchment. Her hair was black as an oil slick, shot through with streaks of silver and piled high atop her head. From her high cheekbones and wide sparkling hyacinth-blue eyes, it was plain that she had once been a beauty before time had its way with her.

"Aladin Ali Ababwa?" The woman scrutinized Yasmina through narrowed eyes, her brow furrowed, a frown tugging at her deeply lined face. "You are his wife? The Sultana?"

Yasmina nodded, her palms sweating. Silence hung between them, more stifling than the heat of the day, until, finally, the woman spoke. "Well, come in, then, child. A friend of Aladin is also a friend of mine. And bring your little friend." The Magi cast her eyes to Banu, who clung to Yasmina's skirts like a shy child. Her face crinkled into a toothless smile as she opened the door to welcome them.

Yasmina glanced around once more to be sure she was not being watched. Upon seeing the empty streets, she slipped through the Seer's door, Banu on her heels. Inside, the entryway was clean but sparse, unornamented, nothing like Yasmina expected the home of a Magi to be. The knot of tension in her spine released a little as she noted no skulls or potions lining the walls. Only a narrow staircase leading up to a second story and two arched doorways to her left and right.

"I had heard that Aladin had gone back to the stars. Do the whispers on the wind speak the truth, child?" the Magi asked softly. Yasmina grimaced as the woman's gaze caught hers, holding it for another beat of silence as Yasmina struggled to release the words that seemed stuck in her throat.

She had not spoken of Aladin, of what had transpired that fateful day in the palace, to anyone. Now, as the buried memories clawed back up to the surface of her mind, grief threatened to choke her and, "Aladin is gone," was all she could manage.

The old woman bowed her head and whispered a quick prayer. "It is as I feared, then. I had hoped I misread the signs. This brings me great sorrow to learn, but not so much, I think, as it brings you. We will speak of this tragedy no more. We will speak of you and what brings you to my door. But not here. Come, child."

The woman gestured to her left, then shuffled through an arched entryway with halting steps. Yasmina and Banu followed, stepping into a dimly lit room with thick curtains drawn against the blazing light of the midafternoon. The room was stifling, and a sheen of sweat broke out across Yasmina's forehead as she looked around.

Again, the room was simple, though there were more signs of the woman's profession here. Tiny glass vials lined crooked shelves on the far wall. Overhead, bundles of plants hung to dry, giving the space an almost overwhelming aroma of mingled flora and herbs that stung Yasmina's nose and burned her throat. A small round table sat in the center, with two wooden chairs on either side. Atop it rested a crystal orb.

The Magi took a seat at the table, motioning for Yasmina to do the same. Noticing the way Yasmina's eyes lingered on the crystal ball, she whispered, "The orb of Anahita knows all. Who you are, who you were, who you wish to become. It sees your deepest secrets and lays bare your greatest fears. But beware. Anahita's answers are not always those we want to hear. What is it you would know, Yasmina Ababwa? What answers have you come here seeking?"

Despite the heat of the day outside, the room seemed to grow colder still as the Magi spoke. Yasmina wrapped her arms around her chest and shivered in her threadbare robes as goosebumps rose on her sweat-dampened flesh. Banu cowered at her feet, clinging to her calf, his nails digging painfully into her skin. Yasmina's heart rate picked up again, thrumming unsteadily, and every impulse in her body told her to flee this place of dark magic.

But she would not... could not.

Instead, she looked up, meeting the Magi's eyes again. "I wish to know how to vanquish Jaffar. I wish to reclaim the throne of Koshagal." Yasmina's voice was low, but she forced herself to keep it steady despite the cold dread building in her veins.

"You are sure? To devote one's life to vengeance, one must often pay a heavy price. There are other paths you might take, easier paths that can be arranged. I could help you leave Koshagal. You are still young, Yasmina Ababwa. You could leave all this behind you and start anew."

Fire replaced the chill in her, and Yasmina gave an aggressive shake of her head. "No. I will reclaim my birthright and avenge my lover. There is no other path for me."

The Magi gave an indifferent shrug. "As you wish. The choice is yours to make." She reached into a small bowl on the table, withdrawing a handful of shimmering dust and sprinkling it over the glass orb. The clouded surface began to clear. "Look, Sultana. See what fate holds for you, if you dare."

Yasmina's hands trembled as she peered into the orb. At first, she saw nothing. She began to wonder if all her seeking had been for naught. Only her own reflection gazed back at her; tangled dark curls covered by a ragged peaked hat. Wide almond-shaped eyes besmirched by the shadows of sleeplessness, a proud aquiline nose.

Then the image inside began to change. Her face twisted and morphed until it was no longer Yasmina's image gazing back but Aladin's. His death mask stared sightlessly out at her, a thin rivulet of blood running down his temple. His cheek was pressed against the cold mosaic tiled floor, eyes gazing sightlessly at nothing. Yasmina reached out for him, a tear gliding down her cheek as she moved to caress his beloved face, knowing it would be cold, knowing he was already dead.

A shudder wracked her as her fingers brushed the surface of the crystal ball, and the image contorted again, becoming the cruelly handsome face of Jaffar. Dark hair, brushing broad shoulders, and onyx eyes, with a sharp, hooked nose. An icy rage sluiced through Yasmina's guts at the sight of him. She wanted to wrap her fingers around the crystal ball and shatter the surface, ridding it of the wicked visage within. She tightened her grip on the orb, squeezing until her knuckles went white as if she could throttle the life from the illusion.

The orb began to burn. Pain lanced Yasmina's hand, and she released it with a gasp as a new face appeared, replacing Jaffar's. An unknown face, yet strangely familiar. She was young and beautiful, with a golden halo crown hovering above silken chestnut locks. Despite never having seen the woman before, Yasmina strangely felt like she had known her all her life.

"Anahita," Yasmina whispered, suddenly recognizing the face of the Goddess of Wisdom.

"You seek your destiny, and so I give it to you. One path of many, but the one you chose." Anahita's disembodied voice resounded through the room, seeming to come from all directions at once. Then her face vanished again, replaced by the gold spires of Koshagal Palace.

"To seek your revenge, you must return from whence you came. Not as who you once were, but as another. You must touch the heart of the man who took your love from you." The voice was high, sharp, inhumanly melodic as Anahita spoke her prophecy.

Yasmina cocked her head and furrowed her brow, confused by the words. "But Jaffar has no heart," she whispered.

"You are wrong. Every man has a heart. And though a Djinn now, Jaffar retains his. And in the darkest depths of that cold, black heart, there is one thing the being you seek to destroy loves and craves above all else. You know what that is, child."

Yasmina hesitated, biting her lip. To think of Jaffar loving anything seemed unfathomable to her at first, but after a moment, the answer came to her. "Power," Yasmina whispered after a long pause.

"Yes. Power. The Djinn will be drawn to power, and his lust for it will be his demise. But be warned—the price of revenge is steep. You might lose more than you gain in the end. Death stalks this path from the shadows."

"Whose death?" Yasmina's voice wavered. She shivered as the shadows in the darkened room seemed to lengthen, reaching out to devour her.

"I cannot say. But this future runs red with blood."

Jaffar's blood, Yasmina hoped, as she sat up straighter and set her jaw. "Whatever the cost, I will pay it."

Anahita's laughter crackled like static through the room. When the goddess spoke again, her voice was a low whisper, quiet as a breeze rustling the branches of an olive tree. "So speak all who believe they have nothing left to lose."

With these last words, the crystal ball went dark. Yasmina stared into the surface, but no further images revealed themselves to her. It was simply a polished crystal orb once more. Lifeless. Inanimate.

She felt a tug at her skirts and blinked down at the monkey desperately clawing at her calves. "Shh, Banu. It is alright," she soothed, then looked up, catching the Magi's eye and holding her gaze.

"I must go back to the palace," Yasmina whispered.

"You are sure? You have been warned there will be a cost to be paid in blood."

"There is no cost I will not pay," Yasmina asserted again, reaching down to collect a still-frantic Banu into her arms. She would have fled the room right then and there for the palace gates if the Magi had not risen and blocked her path.

"Well, you cannot go back like that," the old woman said, shaking her head and frowning. "They will recognize you at once."

Yasmina glanced down at her dusty bare feet and her tattered gown and sighed. The Magi was right. Not only would she be known on sight, but if, by some miracle, she was not, she would never gain entry in her present ragged garb.

"You will need a disguise," the Magi astutely assessed.

Yasmina scowled. "Yes. I suppose I will. But how can I disguise who am I? I have been hunted since I fled. The guards will all know me."

The Seer released a long, world-weary sigh. "Since it seems you will not be swayed away from this path, despite both mine and Anahita's warnings, I will ease it as best I can. To reenter Koshagal Palace, you must become someone else."

Narrowing her eyes, Yasmina peered at the old Magi. "But how?"

The Magi said nothing, only gave Yasmina a stern look that demanded silence, then waved her hands over the crystal ball, drawing a series of intricate patterns over the glassine surface. The air around Yasmina wavered like heat waves on the streets of Koshagal, refracting beneath a midday sun.

The Magi assessed Yasmina, her eyes roving up and down her body. "That is better. Have a look." The old woman gestured at the crystal ball again.

Unsure what to expect, Yasmina stepped closer to the orb and peered into its depths once more. The reflection that gazed back looked a bit like her, yet also not. Her features had been softened. Her face, which had grown haggard from long weeks of hunger, was plump, with voluptuous, pomegranate-tinged lips. Her eyes slanted at an upward angle, her chin narrower, her neck longer and thinner. Her tattered veils were gone, replaced by a simple but elegant bedlah.

She was almost unrecognizable.

"What have you done?" Yasmina whispered, reaching out to touch the image of herself.

"It is only a glamour," the Magi said. The old woman got to her feet and hobbled over to Yasmina. Her face wrinkled into a mischievous grin. She reached around behind Yasmina's neck, fastening a necklace around her throat. Yasmina could feel the pulse of the jade green stone dangling between her full breasts, throbbing in time with her heartbeat.

"The Goddess gives you three weapons with which to seek your revenge. You will need all to overcome Jaffar. This trinket"—the Magi indicated the bauble Yasmina now wore—"is blessed with Anahita's kiss. It will draw the Djinn to you."

The Magi then picked up a tiny steel athame from the table, barely bigger than a darning needle, and handed it to Yasmina. It was unornamented, a simple steel blade small enough for Yasmina to discreetly slip into the hidden pocket she found in her bodice.

"This blade's purpose need not be told, for it speaks for itself. But know that the metal has been thrice enchanted. Even the most powerful Djinn would not live to tell the tale if the blade pierced his heart."

Yasmina swallowed hard. She was no fighter, but if she caught Jaffar off guard, it might be possible...

"And finally," the Magi said, taking Yasmina's hand and placing a small silver pearl in it. "This pearl holds the Tears of Lost Tomorrows."

Yasmina's eyes widened as she stared at the gemstone. It was no bigger than a lentil, smooth and polished, cool against her skin when the Magi placed it in her palm. She had heard of the Tears but thought them little more than a legend. They were a potent poison against the supernatural and need only pass a Djinn's lips to banish them from this world.

The Magi handed Yasmina a small leather pouch, and

Yasmina stashed the potent poison inside and secreted it away beside the dagger.

"Thank you, Magi," she murmured.

The old woman shook her head, looking somber. "Do not thank me, child. These are Anahita's gifts. Use them wisely. Now, go. Seek your destiny at the palace."

Two

YASMINA MADE her way west towards the palace with purposeful strides, her true form masked by the Magi's glamour. By now, the sun was beginning to sink lower on the horizon, the sandstone walls and buildings shifting from gold to bronze in the fading light. As she approached the main palace, Banu tracking her steps all the way, she stepped out of the shading alleys and onto the main thoroughfare that led through Koshagal.

The crowds grew thicker as she drew closer. By the time she reached the palace gates, a riotous, stinking press of bodies surrounded Yasmina. Weak from hunger, she did her best to shove to the front, but it seemed like a vain pursuit. Again, she felt a tug at her skirts and glanced down to see Banu staring nervously up at her, chittering.

"I'm sorry, Banu, but you can't come where I am going." Yasmina patted the little monkey fondly on the head. He gazed mournfully up at her, understanding that this meant goodbye, but seemingly unwilling to accept it. He latched his hands firmly around her ankles. Yasmina shook her leg in a gentle attempt to extricate him from his clinging embrace of her limb.

"If I succeed, we will meet again," Yasmina assured the creature. Her eyes welled with tears she refused to shed. Since Aladin's death, Banu had become her only friend.

The sorrow was painted on Banu's white-masked face as he, at last, relinquished his grip, allowing Yasmina to push unhindered, deeper into the throng headed for the palace.

She *had* to gain entrance. But the crowd was too thick. It carried her where it would, and she was helpless to fight against the wave of the masses. There was little Yasmina could do but ride the tide until it eventually spat her out. The press of sweaty bodies made her skin crawl, the foul odors forcing her to cover her face with hands. She gagged, barely swallowing the bile rising like a tide inside her back down. Then finally, she could breathe again. The crowd had thinned, and Yasmina found herself near the roadside barricade when a rough push from behind sent her sprawling. She stumbled and fell, landing hard on her hands and knees in the middle of the street.

"What do have we here?" a low, faintly amused voice asked.

Yasmina pushed herself up to her hands and knees. A passing caravan had surrounded her, clearly on its way inside the palace. When her eyes rose to the speaker, she had to stifle the gasp that threatened to leave her lips. She found herself staring directly at him... her worst enemy...

Jaffar.

Yasmina trembled, unable to pull her eyes away from his angular, unblemished face. He was handsome in a dark, swarthy way, just as he had been as a man, but even more so now that he was a Djinn. His hair fell in oiled mahogany waves to his shoulders, and his eyes were dark as chips of onyx as they assessed Yasmina where she knelt, collapsed at his feet.

Their eyes were still locked, silently observing one another, when Yasmina felt a slight tugging at her foot. Banu. No. Jaffar could not see Banu. If he recognized the monkey, it would give her away. Yasmina snapped out of her trance, and though it broke her heart to do so, she kicked the little monkey away.

"Go," she hissed through clenched teeth. She did not turn back to see if the monkey had fled into the crowd behind her, but assumed it had, as she no longer felt it clawing at her. She blinked up at Jaffar, trying to regain her composure and take advantage of this unexpected opportunity that had presented itself to her.

"Please, Lord Sultan, forgive me," Yasmina murmured, gazing up at him from beneath the fringe of her thick, dark lashes.

"Careless wretches. How many times must I order you to steer clear of palace gates?" Jaffar snarled. His breath smelled of saffron and tarragon, and the aroma mixed with the cloyingly sweet aroma of his hair oil. He spat in the dirt before her and looked as if he might turn away and resume his procession into the palace.

Then suddenly, Jaffar bent and took Yasmina's chin in his hand, scrutinizing her. Yasmina tried not to flinch away as his nails bit half-moons into her skin. His eyes flicked briefly down to the pulsing amulet at her throat, then back to her face.

"What is your name?" Jaffar asked.

"Jazmin," Yasmina answered, not missing a beat.

Jaffar stroked his perfectly trimmed beard and tilted his head towards her. "And what brings you to the palace, Jazmin?" Jaffar asked, voice smooth as honey. He released her chin and extended his hand to help her up.

"I sought an audience with you, my Lord Sultan." She cast her eyes down, attempting to appear meek and subservient.

Jaffar arched a slender brow at him. "Go on," he said, waving an impatient hand at Yasmina—Jazmin, now.

Jazmin straightened and brushed the dust from her shalvar. "My parents both perished, overtaken by the fever of the rainy season. As a woman alone, with no husband and no home, I'll starve. I hoped you might have a place in your kitchens for a poor orphaned girl..." Yasmina trailed off.

Jaffar shook his head, pursing his narrow lips into a frown, and Jazmin's heart plunged to the dry earth at her feet. This had been her chance, the perfect opportunity. Jaffar's hand released her chin, and she was sure all hope was lost. But instead of casting her aside, he trailed his soft, uncalloused fingertips along her jaw-bone and down her throat, letting them rest on the jewel dangling upon her breast. Jazmin loathed the feeling of desire that heated her with his gentle caress, and barely managed to stifle a shudder of mingled desire and revulsions.

"My kitchens? No." Jaffar scoffed and shook his head. "Not my kitchens. You are far too fine a jewel to leave to rot in my kitchens. No, you belong in my harem, girl." A sly grin spread across Jaffar's face.

Jazmin forced herself not to balk at the offer, plastering what she hoped was a grateful smile across her face.

This was what she wanted, after all. What she needed to do. Revolting as the idea of letting this beautiful but evil man touch her was, nowhere in the palace would allow her to get close to Jaffar so easily as the andaruni that housed the harem.

"I—I would be honored," Yasmina forced out.

Three

⁓

THE GROUND WAS hot beneath Jazmin's feet and pebbles dug into her thin slippers as the guards led her down the twisting path encircling the palace that had once been her home. Paths that she had once walked beside Aladin. The floral scent of the gardens hit her nose, assaulting her with a wave of nostalgia of being there hit her like a gut punch; roses and salvia. Flowers Aladin had once held up for her to scent and tucked behind her ear.

She took a series of deep breaths. In and out. Slow and steady. She was here to avenge Aladin, and her best chance of doing that was to force these memories back, deep down beneath the surface, where they couldn't bubble up and threaten to ruin everything.

Yasmina had never actually been to the andaruni that housed the Sultan's harem. She and Aladin had had no use for a harem, such was their love for one another, and the building had fallen into disuse during their brief reign. Jaffar, however, had wasted no time in reopening it. Aladin's blood had no sooner been wiped from the floors than the women were being recruited for the new Sultan's pleasure house.

Finally, the palace guards stopped before a large door, its broad face etched with scenes of coital bliss that made a touch of color creep into Jazmin's cheeks.

"We go no farther," the tall guard with the scar down his cheek stated, gesturing towards the closed door of the andaruni. "This place is for the Sultan and in his women only. You, you knock." The guards stood at attention, waiting for Jazmin to knock on the door before turning around and walking away.

Jazmin had to take a step back to avoid being hit by the door as it was flung open to reveal a woman with eyes so blue they were nearly violet and flame-kissed, dark hair falling in silky rivulets down to her slender hips. She was older than Jazmin but still quite beautiful.

"You are the new one?" the woman asked, her tone vague and disinterested.

"Yes, I'm Jazmin, Jaffar said—"

"I already spoke to Jaffar about you. I told him his harem is full of beautiful women, and he has no need of a common whore. Yet, you are here." The woman pursed her lips into a sour frown. "I am Daria. First wife of the Sultan and all-powerful Free Djinn Jaffar."

Jazmin's brows shot up in mock surprise. *Play your role,* she reminded herself. *Don't let her rile you. You are just a common woman, hard on your luck. You know nothing of Jaffar, except that he is the Sultan, and was kind enough to...*

"Ah, you did not know the Sultan is a Djinn? The most powerful in the land? You really are a little fool," Daria said with a sneer.

Jazmin had, of course, known that Jaffar was a Djinn. She was just surprised to learn it was common knowledge around the palace.

She followed Daria, who pivoted without another word and strode into the andaruni. She was clad in veils more elaborate than any Jazmin had ever seen, even during her tenure as a Sultana. Likewise, the room was far more opulent than Jazmin's own quarters had been. The walls were mosaiced in elaborate geometric patterns. In the center of the room, a fountain trickled into a small pool full of meandering carp.

Women lounged about the room, eyes focused on Jazmin. As a former Sultana, she was used to the attention. But this was different. There was no adoration in the eyes of these beautiful, painted women, only calculation. She could all but see their minds working. Wondering, was Jazmin a threat? A potential ally? Their furtive glances stayed glued to Jazmin as she followed Daria out of the grand parlor and down a narrow corridor.

They arrived at a small doorway. There was no door, only a long gauzy curtain that Daria yanked aside. She jerked her chin towards Jazmin, indicating she should enter. Not knowing what to expect, Jazmin stepped inside.

The space was tight and unornamented. There was a

small arched window through which a frail rivulet of light trickled. Two chests of drawers, two simple pallets. Nothing more. Still, it was better than the streets, and it got Jazmin within reach of Jaffar.

"This is your room. You share it with Valda, who is around here somewhere. Be prepared at all times for a call from the Sultan. But do not get too comfortable. You would not be the first girl to be dismissed within a moon's cycle."

"Dismissed?" Jazmin echoed.

Daria gave her a tight-lipped smile that didn't reach her eyes. "Yes. Dismissed. Thrown out in the streets like the common, bawdy whore you are." Jazmin flinched from Daria's glare and her sharp words. "Either you please the Sultan, or you'll be gone. Do you understand, slut?"

"I understand," Jazmin forced out past the lump in her throat.

"Good." Daria whipped around and strode out of the room, pulling the curtain closed behind her.

Jazmin stood perfectly still for a moment, waiting for the trembling that had overtaken her body to pass. When the shakiness left her limbs, she crossed the domicile and gazed out the narrow barred window. The sun hung low in the sky now, boiling red in a furious sunset that matched her own mood. Across the gold and scarlet sky, she caught a glimpse of a single white-winged bird cutting across the horizon.

I could have been that bird, she thought. *Flying free,*

somewhere far, far away here. Instead, I find myself caged. Did I choose the wrong path?

Jazmin had no answer to her own question. Right or wrong, it was the road she had chosen to tread. With little else to do, she curled up on the pallet, pulling her knees to her chest. She missed the comforting warmth of Abu's small body curled next to her belly. The monkey was more than just a pet. He was her companion, a friend, and her last living connection to her dead lover. When she closed her eyes and slept, she dreamt of Aladin's gentle touch.

"I've missed you, my love." His fingers trailed over *Jazmin's collarbone, moving up to cup her chin.*

"Aladin, is it really you?"

"It's me, my sweet flower, Yasmina."

Tears overflowed Jazmin's eyes. As they streamed down her cheeks, Aladin reached up, his fingers across the wetness, then bringing them to his lips, licking the tears away. He wrapped his arms around her, pulling her close to him. Warmth radiated from his body into hers as his fingers made their way beneath her veils, trailing down her spine, gripping her narrow hips, and pulling her closer still. She felt his manhood press against her thigh, and a blaze of warmth shot up into her core.

"Welcome home, Yasmina," Aladin whispered in her *ear, his breath tickling her neck.*

Jazmin inhaled, breathing in his scent, and blinked. For but a single moment, her eyes closed. But when she opened them again, Aladin was gone, his face replaced by the cruel sneering visage of Jaffar as he stared down at her, kneeling before him on the road to the palace.

Jazmin awoke with a start, gasping, the mingled bliss and terror of the dream fading only to be replaced by the unsettling sensation of someone watching her. She cracked one eye open. The room was darker than before, evening having fallen while she slumbered. Across the room, another woman lay on her side, chin propped up on her hand, staring at Jazmin with curious brown eyes.

"You're awake."

Jazmin sat up, folding her legs beneath her and blinking sleepily at the girl. She was young, appallingly young, to be in a place such as this, in Jazmin's opinion. But her smile was warm and her voice friendly when she added, "I'm Valda."

"I'm Yesmi..."—she caught herself—"Jazmin."

"You look familiar." Valda squinted at Jazmin, who quickly looked away, blood chilled at the thought of being recognized.

"Unless you frequent the docks on the bayside, I don't see how that's possible," Jazmin responded sharply.

Valda let out a little laugh. "You don't talk like a dock-born peasant." Valda clucked her tongue but, taking the hint, changed the subject. "So, everyone in the andaruni is talking about you. They say you threw yourself at the feet of Jaffar and then enchanted him with a single look."

A blush crept into Yasmina's cheeks. "That's not quite how it happened," she mumbled.

"Well, how did it happen?" Valda pressed. "Tell me the story, the true story, then. There's not much interesting goes on around here."

Jazmin was taken aback by the girl's good cheer. How could she be so airy, so carefree, trapped in this place? *She hasn't lived through the troubles that I have,* Yasmina thought. But no. Jazmin saw the faint scar running down Valda's left cheek and realized that probably wasn't true. More likely, she had seen her share of misery, and this place, with its silks, fineries, bowls of fresh fruit, and overflowing fountains, was a step up from wherever she'd been before.

Jazmin decided to humor the girl. She would give her a story. But as she opened her mouth to begin, she was interrupted by a sharp knock.

"Jazmin," Daria's tone was clipped. She cut an imposing figure, standing tall and straight-backed in the doorway. "Come along, the Sultan begs your attendance."

Valda's jaw dropped open in astonishment as the color slowly drained from Jazmin's cheeks.

"Summoned on your first night! Jazmin, that's a wonder! It never happens. It took me weeks to catch the Sultan's eye," Valda said, sounding awestruck. "Whatever you did, you certainly must have impressed him!"

Jazmin dropped her head under Daria's burning gaze and muttered something noncommittal. Anxiety rose in her like a dark wave. She wasn't ready for this, wasn't ready to face Jaffar. She had been a fool to come here.

"Jazmin," Daria snapped again.

Forcing herself to push the panic deep down inside, Jazmin stood slowly, straightening her veils, and biting her lip.

"I'm ready," she said.

She stared straight ahead, trying to master her breathing, as she followed Daria out of the room.

Four

"COME ALONG. I don't have all day," Daria growled.

Jazmin picked up her pace, following the woman down halls haunted by memories. She had once walked these halls, and the room they, at last, passed into had been Jazmin's own quarters once. Hers and Aladin's. A wave of sorrow washed over her. Aladin, pulling her close, smoothing her hair back away from her forehead. Aladin, touching her as no other man ever had. His strong jaw and boyish smile as he kissed her.

The knot in Yasmina's throat threatened to become a scream. She swallowed it, grinding her teeth into what she hoped was a demure smile as her eyes fell upon Jaffar reclining on a silver-gilt settee, clad in gold chased purple robes. His black hair escaped in soft wisps from his violet silk turban, and his face lit up with a wolfish smile.

"Ah, Jazmin, is it?" Jaffar beckoned with a wave of his hand. "Come closer."

"My Sultan"—Daria stepped between Jazmin and Jaffar—"This one is still covered in filth from the road. Surely you would prefer..."

Jaffar's eyes tracked to Daria. He licked his lips, tongue darting out like a viper's. "Do you question your Sultan's decisions?"

Daria's eyes immediately fell to the floor. "No, my Sultan."

"Then get out of my sight," Jaffar growled.

"Yes, my Sultan."

With that, Daria turned and fled the throne room, and Jaffar returned his attention to Jazmin.

"Step closer," Jaffar repeated, grinning at Jazmin, his teeth sharp and white as opals, his eyes glittering like black shards of onyx.

Jazmin swallowed hard and approached the throne, staring at the floor to avoid meeting Jaffar's gaze.

"Ah, my little street sparrow. So wonderful to lay eyes upon your beauty again."

Jaffar snaked a ring-laden hand out for Jazmin to kiss. She did not hesitate, dipping her head to brush her lips against the uncalloused, bronze skin of his hand.

"Sultan Jaffar, I am honored," she forced out, trying to keep her voice even.

"As you should be. It is not every gutter rat who catches my eye and is offered a space in my harem." The arrogant tone in his voice made Jazmin grind her teeth.

"What does my Sultan wish of me?"

Jaffar's eye caught on the bauble at Yasmina's throat. He gazed at it for a moment, as if enchanted.

"How can I please my Sultan?" Yasmina crooned.

A wicked grin spread across Jaffar's face. His finger beckoned, that wolfish grin spreading wider across his lips. Jazmin drew forward despite every muscle in her body screaming at her to turn and run. She ignored her instincts as she crawled up the settee, her stomach churning with the knowledge of what was to come.

Jaffar's fingers clamped around her throat, right above the chain of the amulet the Magi had given to her. For a moment, panic flared through her at the thought he might yank it from her neck. It wasn't so. Instead, his grip tightened as he pulled her so close, his breath washing over her.

He was nothing compared to Aladin. Her stomach didn't flutter with excitement when she was close. Instead, it twisted and churned, a warning that also went ignored. The pressure on her neck restricted her breaths enough to make them shallow. After a moment, Jaffar released her, sliding those smooth fingers up her neck. They dragged over her flesh, pulled aside the veil of the bedlah that covered her mouth. Goosebumps tingled in their wake. Then he intertwined them in her hair as he pulled her the last few inches until their lips met.

Aladin's kiss been soft, inviting. Jaffar's was cold and rough, just like his demeanor. Still, her lips moved in unison with his. His free hand gripped her waist, pulling her onto his lap. Jazmin straddled him as his fingers gripped her wrists before she could even try to touch him. Jaffar's jaw ticked as he curled his fingers through hers, sharp nails biting into her flesh.

The black jewels of his eyes roamed down her body, assessing the mounds of her breasts, which rose and fell with her unsteady breath. His snake-like tongue once again flicked over his lips, this time hunger in his movements and shimmering in his eyes. After a long moment that felt like the world hung in suspended animation, Jaffer leaned forward and pressed his nose to the nape of her neck. His tongue lashed out, running along the sensitive skin behind her ear. Jazmin's flesh crawled, but the gasp that escaped her own mouth was unwarranted. Her body molded into him involuntarily, slickness growing between her thighs. She wasn't blind. She knew the appeal Jaffar had. He was a striking man, and a practiced lover.

Jaffar released her hands, and Jazmin reached out, her fingers brushing along his robe, hesitant for a moment before pushing them off. Surprisingly, he didn't object, letting her. As the robe fell, his head tilted back, leaving a tingling sensation in the wake of his tongue. Jazmin's eyes trailed down his front, the knot returning to her throat. He was chiseled in all the right places. Her fingers curled into her palms as she struggled to not reach out and touch him, to run her fingers down his chest. Her restraint dwindled as the heat in her core burned, and in a blink, she found herself touching him. Yanking her hand back, she felt a blush creep into her cheeks.

Jaffar's fingers slid up Jazmin's exposed stomach until they reached the edge of the top of her bedlah and pulled it over her head, freeing her breasts. A chill swept down

Jazmin's spine at the sudden exposure. He raked her with his gaze again, the corners of his lips twitching. He looked like he approved, judging from the smug expression on his face. At least, she had to hope it was approval glittering in his eyes. She desperately needed him to want her. It was her only chance of getting close enough to do what needed to be done.

His lips met her neck again, teeth nipping at her flesh. Bitting hard—too hard—before peppering kisses downward and over her breasts. Grabbing her hips with both hands this time, he flipped her over onto the settee, so he was on top. Jazmin had a feeling that he wasn't one to let a woman be on top. Control. With Jaffar, it was all about power and control.

Latching his fingers in the silky skirts Jazmin wore, he pushed them down her legs. As he drew up her body, his fingers returned to her neck and regained their grip, tilting her head back. Her breath hitched as he tightened his fingers harder than before. Her eyes caught his, and a corner of his lips rose in that smirk she wanted to strike from his handsome face.

"You are a beautiful thing," he growled, his hand drifting down, caressing her thigh before his caress trailed inwards.

Her breathing was labored, but her eyes stayed locked with his. Until he dipped his fingers in. He was rough, and yet his touch sent a flurry of emotions through her. He shoved them inside her, not even trying to be gentle, and a ragged gasp left her with slightly parted lips. Jaffar leaned forward, pressing down on her, and instinctively, her hands went to his—fingers digging at him in a futile attempt to pry him off. But she succumbed to his touch as his lips brushed against her ear.

"I may just keep you yet, my little street sparrow," he breathed and pulled his hand away.

Her fingers released his wrist, running down Jaffar's skin in languid circles. He shivered at her touch, unable to deny it. He let go of Jazmin and snatched up her wrists again, small in the grip of his big hands. Raising her arms over her head, he shifted himself between her legs. The head of his cock rested against the inside of her thigh, grazing it.

"Don't move," he warned, teeth clenched.

Jazmin nodded in agreement, but before she could say anything at all, she felt him thrust into her. Her hips bucked at the sudden entrance, and her arms jerked, but he was still holding them hostage, not allowing her to move. With a violent thrust, Jaffar pushed further in, and a moan escaped Jazmin's lips as she tilted her head back.

He was rougher than Aladin. She and Aladin had been equal, but she was submissive to Jaffar, and he made it abundantly clear with his every move. She had no control over Jaffar and had to yield to his yearnings. With Aladin, they had been willing partners, taking their cues from one another.

It didn't help that it was too easy to fall prey to the man on top of her. His chiseled stomach, his bulging muscles. There was no denying the allure of his physique.

It made her insides squirm, making her feel even dirtier than the streets ever had.

His tongue drifted lazily down her breasts, drawing little shapes over them, and sent a fuzzy feeling sweeping through her body. As his mouth grazed downwards, her breath hitched yet again, heart thundering in her ears and ramming against her ribcage. His tongue toyed with the nub of her nipple, pulling out a low moan as her chest heaved. He bit down with his teeth, again too hard, sending a shard of pain through her. He tugged at it and let go, running his tongue between her breasts before taking the other nipple in his mouth, repeating his previous actions. They throbbed with pain as he thrust again, slamming hard into her. His manhood pressed against her walls, delving deep and sending a shudder through her body. Her hips jerked upwards, and they fell into a rhythm as his mouth found hers once more, still hungry.

Jazmin nipped at his lips, inciting a growl deep in his throat. A warning. Their hips crashed against one another. When their lips parted, only gasps filled the air. No tender words of endearment. No sweet nothings whispered. Jaffar's fingers tightened around her wrists again, holding so tight that, after a moment, she couldn't feel her own fingers. He pounded into her, her core tightening with each thrust. She abhorred the desire she felt slicking her thighs. Her body shot through with yearning, tingling sensations sweeping through her. Her thighs tightened, tensing each time he pushed deeper into her.

"Don't," he hissed, the cinnamon and clove scent of his breath washing over her once again. "Only when I say so."

The whimper that escaped her lips was a sound of both reluctance and obedience. Did she dare let his name escape her lips?

It was building, rising inside of her. She was ready to explode, and she loathed that he could stimulate this passion in her. Her fingers tightened around his, her body writhing. She wasn't one to beg, especially not of this man. Jaffar pushed in, his head falling back, eyes rolling heavenward, as he let out a guttural moan. Jazmin's body quivered as she held on, feeling his dick tighten inside of her before releasing.

"Go ahead," he huffed out, barely above a whisper.

Her back arched, slamming their hips together as she let herself explode over him. He groaned at the feeling of her release. Her insides trembled, walls still tight around his dick, but he wasn't ready to pull out. Not yet.

When his eyes opened, bright with the lust that simmered between them, Jazmin stared up at him. Her chest heaved, thighs slick with both of their juices. Her arms went slack, her head thrown back, eyes fixed on the ceiling.

Jaffar's cock twitched, but it was limp inside of her. She could feel it stationary, resting inside of her.

"I may just keep you yet, my little street sparrow." He repeated his previous words, a murmur this time as he laid his forehead on her chest. She felt the faint burn of the pendant, searing heat into the gap between her breasts.

Now? Is this my moment? she wondered, but with her hands clasped in his, there was no way for her to move against him. She would have to wait.

Jaffar's fingers fell away from hers, releasing her from his hold as he pulled out. Jazmin watched as Jaffar drew to his feet and snatched up his gold-trimmed purple robes, slinging them over his shoulders. She didn't miss the way his eyes lingered on the polished jade at her throat. The only thing she still had on.

His turban was askew, and more tufts of black hair tumbled from it, framing his narrow face. Reaching up, he readjusted it and turned, leaving. Her body was still flooded with heat and desire, along with revulsion at letting him so easily control her. Use her.

"Go back with the other girls," Jaffar snapped.

Jazmin inclined her head deferentially. She picked up her bedlah, fingering the hidden pocket containing the blade and the poison. But no, this wasn't the right moment. Next time; she would have to plan better. Use her gifts while she was still pressed up against him.

"Well, what are you waiting for? Out. I have business to attend to."

"Yes, my Sultan," Jazmin whispered, donning the bedlah. Her thighs ached as she left the quarters that had once belonged to her and now housed this monster.

When Jazmin returned to her room, dazed, she collapsed on her pallet, cradling her head in her hands. She tried to hold back the tears, but her anguish was a hot, black pit inside her that she could not climb out of. She broke down.

"Jazmin, what's wrong?" a soft voice asked. Valda. Jazmin cracked one eye open and watched as Valda crawled off her pallet and over to where Yasmina lay weeping. Drawing close, Valda stroked Jazmin's hair and hushed her softly.

"Shhh, was it really so bad? Was it your first time? The first time is always the hardest," Valda whispered.

This only made Jazmin cry harder. Of course it hadn't been her first time. Her first time had been with Aladin. Gentle, sweet-natured Aladin who had treated her like a porcelain doll that first time, every stroke gentle, inching into her bit by bit, whispering, "Are you okay? I'm not hurting you, am I?" Aladin had never hurt her, not even for a moment.

With Jaffar, it was all about power. His power over her. His thinly veiled brutality.

Jazmin choked on her sobs, hiccuping out shaky breaths as tears mingled with snot and ran down her face. Ugly crying.

"Hush now. It will be alright. It isn't so bad after a while. You'll get used to it," Valda murmured, massaging Jazmin's shoulders.

Jazmin's head snapped up. When her gaze met Valda's, her eyes were so full of fury and hatred that the girl froze, then flinched away.

"I will never get used to it," Jazmin said slowly, enunciating each word. "I will make sure he never does it to you or me again," she vowed.

Valda sighed. She took Jazmin's face in her hands and wiped the tears from her cheeks. Then she pulled her close in an embrace that was strong and tender and reminded Jazmin of Aladin's. She melted into it, pressed her head against Valda's chest. Too weary to weep anymore, she, at last, fell asleep.

Five

~

SUNS ROSE, and the moons set over Koshagal. As the days passed, neither Valda nor Jazmin was summoned by Jaffar, and things fell into something of a routine. Jazmin had not expected to make a friend in the andaruni, but it was hard not to like Valda, and they shared something in common. As the two newest concubines, both girls were shunned by those of higher rank. Every morning, Jazmin woke, feeling empty inside, though. She thought of Abu often. Was Aladin's monkey still out there, surviving? She hated to think he was all alone. But then, so was she.

Jazmin was lonely, and when her loneliness began to eat away at her, Valda was always there.

During the day, they wandered the gardens and enclosures, talking about their lives before the andaruni. Valda did most of the talking, with Jazmin chiming in with short answers, feeling guilty that all she told the girl was lies.

"I was the daughter of the harbormaster," Valda explained one day as they sat outside in the courtyard lying beneath the gnarled branches of a large pomegranate tree. "When I was a child, we were so happy. We had everything we could ever want. Then Jaffar came into power. The taxes kept getting higher and higher. Soon my family was left with nothing. My father had no way to feed us, clothe us." She paused, taking a deep breath, sorrow flickering in her eyes. "In the end, he threw himself into the sea."

"I'm so sorry. He took so much from so many." Jazmin reached out and rested her hand on Valda's shoulder, pulling her into an embrace.

Valda buried her face in Jazmin's shoulder, her tears moistening her skin. Rubbing her back, Jazmin soothed her. "We can't go back," she whispered. "We can only press on." The words were ash in her mouth. Oh, how she wished they could both just go back. Back to the happy past they'd both known.

She reached down and took Valda's chin in her hand, so they were gazing into each other's eyes. And something stirred inside her. Something she'd thought had disappeared the moment the light went out in Aladin's eyes. *Desire.*

She smelled of rosewater and ylang-ylang, her skin smooth and supple beneath Jazmin's fingertips. As their gazes held, Valda leaned in. Their lips brushed in a whisper-soft kiss that tasted of honey and tea leaves.

"Oh," Jazmin whispered as she pulled away, opening

her eyes and gazing at Valda, who sat motionless with slightly parted lips.

"I'm sorry. I should not have—" A furious blush crept into Valda's cheeks, and she averted her eyes, staring at the dusty earth of the courtyard.

Jazmin held a hand up, silencing the girl's protest. "Don't be sorry," she whispered.

Valda's eyes drifted up to meet Jazmin's. Both held hunger. And shame. This was forbidden. Not by the laws of the Gods, no. But by Jaffar, who styled himself as a ruler above the Gods. This was dangerous, but Jazmin did not care. Valda's soft kiss had filled a hole that had been inside her since Aladin's death. A dark chasm someone like Jaffar could never fill.

And so it went for more settings of the sun. The two women, stealing kisses when no one was looking. But it was by night that their love bloomed. Tentative at first, but soon they were practiced in their passions towards one another. Fingers and tongues created a passion unlike any Jazmin had ever known. She hadn't thought she would be able to love again, let alone love a woman. But Valda emitted an aura that brought peace to Yasmina's tortured soul. In her arms, she forgot about the loss of her throne. She didn't think about Jaffar.

She almost managed to forget the loss of Aladin.

Still, when Valda fell into a contented sleep each night, Jazmin fingered the silver dagger in her bodice and rolled the small poisoned pearl between her fingers until she, at last, fell into a slumber laced with dreams of revenge.

All things end, and so too did this brief flash of contentment Jasmine and Valda found in each other's arms. The whispers of their love affair passed from one set of jealous lips to another. Jazmin heard the sniggers and murmurs more every day until, finally, they found the ear of the First Wife.

Outside, the light was fading, a gold and slate gloaming settling over the sliver of horizon visible through their narrow window. Jazmin and Valda lay on Jazmin's bedroll, their bodies naked and gleaming copper in the waning light of the sun.

"You are the sunset to me," Valda whispered, trailing her fingers along Jazmin's belly, tracing the orb of her navel, then coming to rest on her inner thigh. "Beautiful and bright, different every time. Sometimes fiery and vibrant, but not tonight. Tonight you are the sky before a storm.

A faint smile crossed Jazmin's lips as she drew back from the dark thoughts that haunted her mind. It had been weeks since Jaffar had called her to his chambers. How was she to kill the man, the Djinn, if she could not get close to him?

She blinked away the last vestiges of her frustration, moving her hand to cup Valda's breast. Her fingers moved in languid circles, tracing the aureola until the nipple puckered and hardened with yearning. "And you are my moon goddess. The beauty that rises in my sky every night."

Valda laughed. "I am no moon. The moon is cold and round and oh so far away. I am slender, warm, and right here with you." Valda snuggled close, twining her legs with Jazmin's, so their thighs pressed against one another.

Grinning, Jazmin squeezed Valda's firm ass with one hand. "You are round here." She gently pinched her supple breast with the other. "And here."

Valda giggled, swatting at Jazmin's hands playfully. She caught one and brought it to her lips, kissing each knuckle lightly. Then she pulled her closer. Their mouths met, tongues probing. Valda's fingers trailed up Jazmin's inner thigh. They found the rosebud of her womanhood and began caressing it with smooth, quick motions. Jazmin let out a low moan, tangling her fingers in Valda's hair.

And then they both froze as Daria's voice boomed into their chamber.

"What is this sacrilege?" Daria demanded, staring aghast at the naked, entwined forms of Jazmin and Valda lying upon the pallet.

The First Wife stormed into the room, grabbing Valda roughly by the arm and hauling her to her feet. She flicked her eyes to Jazmin. Cold eyes. Eyes as void of compassion and empathy as Jaffar's.

Then she turned back to Valda, raising her right hand and smacking her hard across her face with the back of it. The slap resounded through the silent chamber, and Valda crumpled to the floor, blood blossoming from a gash where one of Daria's rings had cracked across the bridge of her nose. Daria still held her in her grip, with Valda's arm wrenched upward at an unnatural angle.

Jazmin leaped to her feet, covering her sex with one hand and her breasts with the other. Her heart pounded a furious drumbeat in her ears.

"How dare you?" she snarled, baring her teeth, half-feral with rage as she stormed towards Daria.

"Jazmin, don't!" Valda cried.

Valda's voice brought her back to herself. The red haze of rage over her vision cleared, and her blind fury lifted. She dropped her hands to her sides, breathed a ragged sigh, and took a single, measured step towards Daria.

"Let her go," Jazmin ordered in a low snarl. It was not the voice of Jazmin, the street urchin and harem girl, but the commanding tone of Yasmina, the once-ruler of Koshagal. Yasmina, the Sultana.

Daria's eyes met Jazmin's. It seemed she did not like what she saw in that burning gaze. With a grunt, she released Valda's arm. The younger girl whimpered, rubbing her dislocated shoulder as she sat dazed upon the floor.

"Get dressed now. You will both be coming with me," Daria said, her voice trembling. She turned and stormed out of the room, her body trembling with barely concealed fury.

"Oh, Gods." Valda's voice cracked, tears streaming down her face as she collected her bedlah with shaking hands and began donning it. "Jaffar will kill us. He'll mount our heads on the palace walls."

Jazmin shook her head. "He won't."

Valda looked up at her, the tears making her eyes bright. "Jazmin, you don't understand," she protested.

Jazmin didn't respond. Instead, she reached for her own bedlah and put it on silently. Slipping her hand into the bodice, she pulled out the hidden knife, brandishing it at Valda.

"Jazmin, you can't. He's a Djinn!" Valda whispered furtively, but Jazmin paid her no mind as she slipped out the door of the chambers.

Her time had finally come.

Daria waited outside the door. She cast a scowl at both of the wayward girls, then barked, "Come with me." She stalked through the corridors of the palace, Jazmin and Valda trailing her a few feet behind until she burst into Jaffar's throne room.

Jaffar lounged on his throne. His purple robes were thrown open, revealing his sculpted abdomen. Two girls, vaguely familiar to Jazmin from the andaruni, stood on either side of him, bearing bowls of dates, figs, and olives. His dark eyes narrowed as they shifted from Daria to Valda, then finally landed on Jazmin.

"What seems to be the problem, Daria?" Jaffar drawled, picking up an olive in his perfectly manicured fingers and popping it into his mouth.

Daria cleared her throat, folding his arms across his chest. "I caught these two fondling one another in the andaruni," she accused in an acid tone.

"Oh, really?" Jaffar licked his lips, appraising the two girls. Valda's eyes were downcast, blood still flowing from the wound on her face. Yasmina leveled a gaze so hateful at him that his eyebrows shot up, startled.

"Leave us, Daria. I shall punish them."

"But Sultan, as First Wife, it is my duty to mete out their senten—"

Jaffar glowered at her. He drummed his beringed fingers on the arm of the gold chair, the muscle in his jaw working as his teeth ground into a frown.

"As your Sultan and your husband, my authority overrules yours," Jaffar declared. "The women are mine to punish as I see fit."

Daria opened her mouth to protest, then slammed it closed, glaring at Jaffar a moment longer before her face collapsed into a sulky pout. Grudgingly, she trudged from the throne room, slamming the door behind her as she went.

Jaffar redirected his attention to Jazmin and Valda. He gazed at them placidly, drumming his long-nailed fingers on his thigh, stroking his beard with one hand.

"So, what to do with you two harlots?" he mused. "Have you anything to say for yourselves? Surely, you know I have forbidden my girls from lying with others. And that includes each other." His eyes flicked from one girl to the other, landing on Jazmin and lingering there.

"My Sultan—" Valda began, but Jazmin cut her off.

"Back up," Jazmin hissed at Valda through clenched teeth. The girl didn't listen. Instead, she shook her head and reached for Jazmin's hand.

Jazmin gave her a stony look and shoved her lover away, hard.

With a whimper, Valda fell to the mosaic stone floor behind Jazmin, who touched her amulet. It pulsed at her throat, and the glamour fell away as she peeled off the veil from her face. And there stood Yasmina.

Not Jazmin the whore or Yasmina, the bedraggled barefoot street urchin in soiled robes. No. Yasmina, the bright-eyed, headstrong princess, stood before Jaffar. And Yasmina lusted for revenge and the Djinn Sultan's blood above all else.

"Sultana," Valda gasped, her eyes wide with wonder as she watched the transformation complete before her eyes.

"The prodigal daughter returns," Jaffar said amicably with a sharp bark of laughter. "I knew there was something familiar about you."

The amulet pulsed again, and Yasmina noticed Jaffar's eyes fixed on it.

"That trinket," he murmured, rising to his feet and striding towards her. Yasmina was vaguely aware of Valda calling out her name. Not her true name, Yasmina, but Jazmin, the one she'd invented. But her world had narrowed. There was only her and Jaffar now. Nothing else mattered. Nothing else existed.

"You killed Aladin. You stole my throne. I am here to reclaim what is mine," she hissed.

Jaffar laughed again and moved towards her with inhuman speed, his Djinn powers suddenly apparent as he lunged for Yasmina's throat with his clawed fingers. Yasmina dodged him, barely, and reached into her bodice. She had just wrapped her fingers around the hilt when Jaffar grasped her wrist in his fingers.

Suddenly, her hand felt cold. Her fingers seized up, releasing their grip on the blade. Icy pinpricks streaked through her arm, and it fell immobile to her side.

Poison touch. A Djinn power.

She could feel the magic crawling through her. She grasped her shoulder and collapsed, pain lancing through her.

Jaffar cackled and kicked her hard in the ribcage. Yasmina coughed, struggling to breathe as Jaffar changed targets, approaching Valda.

"And you, the dockmaster's wench. What's your role in this?" he growled.

"Nothing," Yasmina gasped through the pain in her ribs. "She is innocent of all but befriending me."

Jaffar snorted. "An innocent whore? That would be a first."

Valda surprised them both, rising to spit in Jaffar's eye, then grabbing for him, raking her nails down his throat, drawing blood. Jaffar's handsome face contorted, turning purple with rage. He grabbed Valda by the hair and howled, smashing her head down against the tile floor with his inhuman strength.

The scene was so eerily reminiscent of the night Jaffar had killed Aladin that Yasmina felt bile rise in her throat.

She forced herself to her knees. The poison had not reached her left side yet, though she could feel its slow crawl through her veins. She reached into her bodice and pulled the dagger free. It felt awkward and unwieldy in her off hand, but she knew this was her only chance to save Valda, to depose Jaffar, to avenge Aladin.

Her hand shook as she lifted her arm and hurled the blade through the air. It grazed Jaffar's back. Not a killing wound. Not through the heart. But it was enough to distract him. Jaffar let Valda's body fall to the floor and turned to roar at Yasmina.

"You vile bitch! I should have killed you when I had the chance, when I killed your lover. *Aladin*. Stupid fool of a street urchin." He paused and smirked. "Just. Like. You are now," he enunciated slowly.

This was it, Yasmina realized. This was the end. She had failed. She had failed to reclaim her throne. She had failed to avenge Aladin. And worst of all, she had failed to save Valda, who lay with eyes staring sightlessly up at the ceiling, body faintly twitching.

Yasmina forced her body to respond despite the chill overwhelming it. She reached into her bodice. Shaking, she struggled to open the drawstring pouch and shake the poisoned pearl free from it.

"What are you doing over there?" Jaffar snarled, streaking across the room towards Yasmina.

Yasmina desperately reached up and popped the pearl in her mouth with the last of her strength before her left side began to seize up.

When Jaffar reached her, she surprised him. Instead of fleeing, she reached out, grabbing him by his robes, and pulling him close. She leaned forward, bringing her face close to his, pressing her mouth to his. The pearl hovered on her tongue. She could taste the acid bite of its poison. As her tongue danced between his lips, she spat it out into his mouth.

Jaffar gazed at her, first bemused, then horrified, as the poison pearl began dissolving in his mouth. He raised his fist to strike Yesmina, but before he could, his body seized, jerking wildly. Collapsing to his knees, plumes of gray smoke poured from the Djinn's mouth, and his skin turned a putrid shade of green.

"You harpy. You wretch! No, this cannot be!" Jaffar lamented, clutching at his throat with his fingers. The flesh had begun to flake away, leaving skeletal claws where his hands had once been.

The sounds of his cries became muddy in Yesmina's ears, and in the last moments before the black crept into the edges of her sight, she saw a puff of smoke. Jaffar was gone. Her arch nemesis vanquished, but the victory was a bitter one.

Yasmina crumpled to the floor, sobbing as pain and numbness. She could feel the poison rushing in her bloodstream. The Djinn magic. The residue from the pearl. Her vision blurred, split in two, and wavered. Shudders wracked her immobile body.

Her eyes strayed to Valda's prone body, and a deep sorrow filled her whole being. This wasn't what she wanted. For revenge, she would have gladly sacrificed her own life. But Valda? Sweet, innocent Valda. She was helpless to do anything but scream, the long, high-pitched keen of mourning pouring from her throat. Eyelids fluttering, the world began to go dark around her except for one small pinprick of light that grew and swelled until it became a form in the impenetrable darkness.

Jaffar, was Yasmina's first thought, *coming back to mock me in my failure.*

But as the figure emerged from the blinding lightness, she realized it was not Jaffar. It was a man, but his slender feline grace was nothing like the Sultan-Djinn's broad stature and chiseled musculature.

"Come, my beloved, my sweet flower. Close your eyes, rest. We need never be parted again," a familiar voice filled the dark silence.

"Aladin?" Yasmina whispered, hoarse.

The figure crouched beside Yasmina and he drew a finger to his lips, hushing her.

"Sleep. Sleep now, Yasmina," he said in his dear, deep voice. "We have a hundred thousand lifetimes together now."

Then another figure appeared beside him. Long dark hair, a heart-shaped face, and a smile Yasmina would recognize anywhere. Valda.

"Your battle is won, Sultana. Come home with us."

Yasmina's paralyzed muscles twitched one last time before blackness swept over her.

Yasmina slept.

Six

THE FEELING of warmth upon her cheek. Sunlight streaming through a window, falling upon her brow. Yasmina's eyes opened slowly, the sudden brightness causing stars to float against the scrimshawed shadow and light. She blinked, her vision clearing enough to make out a small form scurrying up to her.

"Banu," she whispered, her voice hoarse. "How did you get here?" For Yasmina thought, surely she was safe in the afterlife. Had the little monkey perished, just had she had, wandering the streets of Koshagal alone?

Banu waved a paw towards the open window, a cool evening breeze making the curtains flutter, and suddenly Yasmina was confused as her eyes began to make sense of the space around her. The bronze sconces upon the walls, the turquoise and gold of the mosaic tile floor. Why was she still in the throne room? The next world could not so perfectly resemble her home, could it?

Panic crept into her voice. "Where did Aladin go? And Valda? They were both here..."

The monkey gave her a strange look and shook his head, twittering incoherently and smoothing Yasmina's hair with his tiny fingers. She pushed up off the cold floor to a seated position, barely able to make her body obey her commands, and looked around as the monkey climbed into her lap.

There was no sign of Aladin, but as Yasmina's eyes scanned the silent room, they fell on the Valda.

Her slight form was sprawled on the cold tile floor. Her head was tilted to one side at an unnatural angle. A thin trickle of blood dripped from her nose, streaking down the side of her face. Her golden skin had paled and lost its luster, bruise-blue where the flesh pressed against the cold floor.

"No," Yasmina whispered. "Please, no." She tried to stand but lacked muscle control, the poison still lingering in her system. Undeterred, she clawed at the floor, dragging herself using only her arms, like a baby just learning to crawl, towards her friend and lover's body.

Banu protested, placing himself between Yasmina and Valda. He gave her a solemn shake of the head, but Yasmina continued forcing herself forward, nails snapping as she went, fingertips bleeding as they clawed at the floor.

"I have to help her," she muttered over and over, though she knew, in her heart, it was too late. Valda's eyes were wide open and unblinking. She was already gone.

Yasmina reached for Valda, lacing her fingers with her

lovers. They were cold already, the skin rubbery, the flesh stiff and heavier than it had been in life. Yasmina squeezed her hand all the same as if this simple act could once again force blood to flow through her veins. Memories hit her like the Kaspian's breaking waves crashing against the white-sanded shore during a storm. Valda's fingers on her thigh. Aladin's fingers in her hair. Ghosts of those she's lost tugging at her heart.

Her muscles gave out, and she collapsed, cheek pressed against Valda's stiff hand.

Time passed. The light filtering in through the windows of the day diminished, and long shadows crept across the floor, growing closer to Yasmina. She wished they would reach out and grab her, pull her back to the underworld where those she loved were locked away forever, without her.

But they did not. Instead, a voice sounded from the entrance of the throne room.

"Jaffar, my Sultan?"

Yasmina looked up, the tension in her neck loosening. A man stood in the doorway, with a white beard, carrying the bejeweled staff of a vizier.

"Jaffar is gone." Yasmina's voice rang out in the room. She forced her body to betray her, rising slowly to her feet.

The man's eyes widened, and he shook his head in disbelief. "Yasmina? Can it be?"

She stood on shaking limbs, her lips set in a thin, grim line. Banu's arms wrapped around her calf, clinging to her.

Taking a deep, wavering breath, she declared, "I have vanquished the Djinn and reclaimed my birthright. I am the daughter of the Sultan, wife of Aladin Ali Ababwa, may his spirit rest forever in the stars. The throne of Koshagal belongs to me

She hoped the words sounded less hollow than she felt. The emptiness and sorrow stretched out inside her, seeming to fill every organ, as the Magi's words repeated in her head. *'The price of revenge is steep.'* *Too steep,* Yasmina thought.

The vizier dropped to his knees before her. Behind him, more of the palace denizens began to trickle in. As they stepped through the wide arched doorway into the throne room and their eyes fell upon their prodigal Sultana, they too fell prostrate before her.

"Prepare a royal burial for Valda." She gestured to the corpse of her lover but did not look at Valda. She could not do so without breaking down.

The grey-haired vizier lifted his head and stared at her. "But, Your Majesty, she was only a harem girl. Royal burials are reserved for—"

"She was an innocent," Yasmina barked, "and she died for my own foolish vanity and thirst for vengeance. A royal burial. And bring me the First Wife's head on a spike."

And so her reign began, with blood and tears.

About the Author

Author Bio

Kate's writings interweave fantasy and mythology into unique, romantic tapestries. An introvert, dog mom, and freelance editor, when she's not searching for fairy circles in hopes of being transported to an enchanted kingdom, Kate is immersed in the chaos of her writing process.

She lives with her husband and her rescue dog Gracie on the banks of the Hudson in Westchester County, NY, where, alas, she has found few portals to magical Realms.

Links:

Facebook group: www.facebook.com/groups/Courtofdreams

Facebook page: www.facebook.com/katesegerauthor

Instagram: www.instagram.com/katesegerauthor

Tiktok: https://www.tiktok.com/t/ZTd3txyDD/